RESIDUAL WASTE

Norman Burslem

ARTHUR H. STOCKWELL LTD
Torrs Park, Ilfracombe, Devon, EX34 8BA
Established 1898
www.ahstockwell.co.uk

British Library Cataloguing-in-Publication Data.
A catalogue record for this book is available
from the British Library.

By the same author:
Nits and Other Afflictions

For their help and support, to my friends Louise
Spendelow-Wrench and Oliver Gallagher.
Best wishes from Norman Burslem.

ISBN 978-0-7223-4922-9
Printed in Great Britain by
Arthur H. Stockwell Ltd
Torrs Park   Ilfracombe
Devon EX34 8BA

CHAPTER 1

It was Monday morning and it was raining. Jack Sugden arrived at Chelford Town Recycling Centre, better known locally as The Tip, to find his colleague Mollie Knowles waiting for him.

"Thank God you're here, Jack – the rain is beginning to run down my neck; Simon has had to take our car in for a service."

"Get in my car, Mollie, while I open up. There's one good thing about rain, because it means we won't have too many clients this morning at least."

Mollie squeezed herself into the Ford Fiesta while Jack searched for his keys.

"Jack, you haven't forgotten that we have those two new blokes starting today, have you?"

Jack had forgotten, but he wasn't about to admit it.

"Yeah, that's right; now just remind me of their names."

"There's a Dimitri Rotarescu and Winston Green."

"Dimitri what? He's not British, surely?"

"Probably not, Jack."

"He's another one come over here taking one of our jobs, then."

"Well, if you remember, Jack, the council has had problems finding anyone to fill the posts."

Jack knew this to be true because he had been moaning for weeks about being understaffed.

"Winston Green sounds OK though, Mollie."

"Well, Jack, I understand from his file that he is of West Indian descent although he was born and brought up in Brixton."

3

Jack attempted a joke as he made to leave his vehicle: "That means, Mollie, that there will be two of them who don't speak English fluently – not like us, eh, duck?"

Jack Sugden had risen through the ranks and now held the title of recycling supervisor at Chelford town tip; Mollie Knowles was his administrator. She spent her days in the Portakabin which served as an office complete with Internet connection. Mollie's first job today was to make two cups of tea while Jack parked his car.

The Tip opened for business at 9 a.m., so they had time for a quick cuppa before any customers arrived. Today, however, two young men appeared at the Portakabin door before they could even sip their tea. Mollie knew immediately that the new recruits had arrived.

"Come in, gentlemen, please."

The twosome presented a complete contrast: one was tall, smartly dressed and extremely handsome; the other was short and rather scruffy.

"Thank you very much, lady," the tall one said.

"Have a seat, lads, while I find Mr Sugden. He's the boss."

Mollie saw Jack leave the Gents toilet cabin, which was situated at the edge of the staff car park.

She opened a side window and called out, "Mr Sugden, Mr Sugden, the new lads have arrived."

Jack hurried over to the office; both men stood up as he entered. The taller of the two towered over him.

"Good morning, sir. I am Dimitri Rotarescu."

The shorter man also announced himself: "Hiya. I'm Winston."

Jack Sugden felt a crick in his neck as he looked from one to the other.

"Right, sit down, lads, while I explain the importance of our work here; then I will take you on a tour of the compound."

"I'll make some more tea, shall I, Jack, while you explain things?"

"Er, yes, thank you, Mrs Knowles." Jack now felt more in charge with the newcomers sitting below his eyeline, so he began his explanation: "You have gained employment in a most important facility which caters for a wide area. We take a range of garbage, but exclude asbestos and plasterboard for obvious reasons. I have a staff of five people, two of whom are yourselves. When we have drunk our tea I will show you round the facility and point out the various containers, all of which have large signs informing our customers of what can be deposited in them. Part of your job is to ensure that customers deposit their rubbish in the correct containers. We are held accountable for accurate depositing and our wages can be cut if mistakes are made. Do you understand what I am saying?" Both newcomers nodded to show their understanding, so Jack continued his discourse: "Occasionally we have problems with customers who think they know more than us about rubbish disposal. Now, if you come across any such person or persons you refer them to me immediately; is that understood?"

Once again two heads nodded.

"Now, do you have any questions?"

Winston Green had a query: "What's the rate of pay, Mr Sugden?"

"You will be paid the national minimum wage providing you make no mistakes."

Dimitri Rotarescu also needed enlightenment: "How many hours must we work each week, please, sir?"

"We work a five-day week, which includes Saturday and Sunday but we have Wednesday and Thursday free."

Dimitri had another question: "Can I seek other work on my days off, please, sir?"

"Yes, as long as you turn up here on the appointed days. Actually, son, you'll be lucky to find another job around here at the present time."

"That's a shame, sir, because I must send money back to support my family in Romania."

"Well, you might be lucky – the Town End Care Home sometimes needs temporary staff. But now let's go out so I can show you the ropes."

The newcomers rose to follow Jack, but the trio were interrupted because Mollie arrived with the tea.

"I've put some biscuits on this big plate for you all."

They all sat down again to enjoy the snack, and Jack's plan received a further setback because his two other permanent staff members appeared at the office door.

"Eh, don't wolf down all them biscuits; me and Pete need a couple." The speaker was middle-aged and dishevelled; his large body almost covered up a second figure, who was younger and slimmer but equally scruffy.

Jack did the introductions: "Right, Fred and Pete, here's our new colleagues." He pointed at Dimitri and Winston, who were still seated. "This is . . . er . . . what's your name again, son?"

Dimitri stood up to answer: "I am Dimitri Rotarescu from Bucharest."

The worker named Pete was puzzled: "Bucha what, mate?"

"Bucharest. It's in Romania."

"'Ere, that's in Stoke, isn't it – near Etruria?"

Dimitri did not understand, so he remained standing but silent.

Winston now took the opportunity to announce himself: "Hiya, I'm Winston Green and I'm from Brixton."

Pete smiled at him. "I've been there on 'oliday, mate; it's near Torquay, ain't it?"

By now Jack had had enough: "Right, guys, it's time for work, but before I open the main gate I must just introduce our oldest expert to our new lads." He pointed at the elderly biscuit seeker. "This is my second in command, Fred Urmston; he's worked here for nearly twenty years and he knows all the ropes. And standing somewhere behind him is Pete Fenton. Right, it's opening time, so I'll unlock the main entrance; Fred, you show the new lads the ropes; Pete, you get ready to help our first customers; and, Molly, check when that firm is coming to pick up the small appliances."

Fred beckoned Dimitri and Winston. "Follow me, lads."

The Tip was arranged as a circle; customers could drive in, provided their vehicle was a car or a small van, and park alongside various large containers, which could be accessed on foot up steep metal ramps. Each container had a large notice facing the parked vehicles. Dimitri noticed depositories for garden waste, mattresses, cardboard, small electrical items and residual waste. The last-named confused him.

He turned to Fred: "Excuse me, sir, but what is this container for?"

Fred took several seconds before he realised that, for the first time in his life, someone had knighted him.

"Oh, right, well, it's for rubbish that can't be recycled. Jack, our boss, supervises this container because some lazy customers dump anything in it; you don't have to worry because Jack watches what goes in it like a hawk. Now see the container for small appliances over there."

Dimitri and Winston turned and looked in the direction indicated by Fred's dirty index finger.

"You don't have to worry about that one either; Pete supervises that one."

Winston was puzzled. "So what do you want us two to do, then, Fred?"

"Right, you wait in the parking area and when people get out of their cars you offer them help. Look out for the elderly because they find the ramps very steep."

"But, sir, what happens when many cars arrive together?"

"Well spotted, Dimi; so you wait for people to approach you for help. Now, if you're not sure where their rubbish goes, come and ask me or Pete, OK?" Both newcomers smiled; everything seemed very straightforward.

Dimitri's first customer was female; she stopped by the garden-waste container. She was youngish, probably in her thirties, and very shapely.

Dimitri approached her vehicle: "Madam, can I assist you?"

The woman looked him up and down; in her mind she thought, 'Yes, love, I'm sure you can.'

But she said, "Could you help me with this garden stuff, please?"

"Yes, of course, madam."

She opened the boot and at that exact moment her toddler in the back seat burst into tears.

"Don't worry, madam, I'll clear your car; your baby needs you, I think."

She took the baby from its security seat and walked over to where Jack was standing.

"Eh, Jack, where did you find young Tarzan?"

"Oh, hello, Clare. Yeah, he's new – first day on the job. He's foreign, of course, but the other lad is English."

"Well, Jack, I would say the foreigner will be a big attraction for some I could name."

"You could be right, Clare, but for me the main thing is he sticks with the job – I'm fed up with young blokes starting and then chucking it in after a few weeks. I had two walk out last Saturday – left us in a right mess, they did."

By now The Tip was becoming busier, with cars and vans queuing by the main entrance.

"Right, Clare, I've got to go – customers are piling in."

June Bailey, matron at the Town End Care Home, was faced with a new problem. Over the weekend she had received a delivery of some new mattresses. Residents at the care home frequently ruined various items of bedding – so much so that June often had to pay the local council to remove soiled and damaged bedding. In the recent past this had been no problem, but now the council had put up its rates for disposal while simultaneously lowering its financial support for some of the care homes' residents. June had to work within a strict budget, and today she was faced by a mountain of plastic wrapping that had protected twelve new mattresses and she did not have a plan for its disposal; however, undeterred, she called one of her senior staff into her office on this wet Monday morning.

"Sami, we need to get rid of all that plastic. Have you any ideas how we can do it without incurring any costs?"

Sami Barroti grimaced at her, but then his expression changed.

"How about this, Matron: I pack the plastic into the home's estate car and take it to the local tip? I mean, they're bound to take plastic wrapping, aren't they?"

"I'm not sure, Sami, but it's worth a try. But don't go in your uniform; go as though you're a local householder."

"Can I take Imran to help me, Matron?"

"No, because we may made need to use the ruse many times in the future and I don't want to raise the council's suspicions. The Tip is bound to be covered by CCTV, so, if you do it this time, Imran can do it on another occasion; however, you can instruct him to help you load the car. If you do it early today you may be the only one there at The Tip."

"Right, Matron, I'll get it done right away."

She followed Sami out of the office because it was time to ensure that all the residents had had breakfast. On her way to the dining room she met one of the newer and fitter residents.

"Why, good morning, Mr Weston. You're up bright and early and you're ready to go out, I see."

Basil Weston had moved in a few months ago after the death of his wife; he was in his mid seventies, and apart from high blood pressure he was pretty fit. Dr Priest had suggested that he walk every day for forty minutes or so.

"It's stopped raining now, Matron, so I thought I'd nip into town – no, not nip, slouch might be more accurate."

June smiled at him – it was good to have someone with full mental faculties with whom she could share a joke.

"Well, wrap up warm – and no smoking! Remember what Dr Priest told you."

"Right you are, Matron. Now, I'll be back in time for morning coffee."

During his short time at the care home Basil had developed a coping method – the other residents were much more infirm than he was and most were hard to communicate with. They spent most of their days in the main lounge. Basil found the room to be very depressing, so he spent as much of the day as possible out around town. He did enjoy a cigarette and the odd pint of beer, but to avoid staff telling him off he had to indulge himself well away from the care home. Today he followed his normal practice: he walked slowly towards the town centre along Church Walk, which was level for 200 yards or so; then, in front of the church building it became an upward slope which ran alongside the main road and its name changed to Church Terrace. By now it was ten or so feet above the roadway and there were two wooden benches. Normally Basil sat on the one closer to the town centre, but today it was occupied by a young couple he had never seen before. This really was not a problem: Basil sat on the other bench and fished out a cigarette from deep within his overcoat. He planned to stay put until the town pub opened, then he would indulge himself with a pint of bitter. He was on his third puff when the young couple burst into laughter. Basil looked over to the other bench and saw that they were both gazing at one of those newfangled smartphones. He guessed they were both in their late teens, though the boy could have been older. Suddenly the male looked away from the phone and turned his head towards Basil.

"What do you think you're starin' at, Granddad?"

Basil was caught completely off guard, but he did manage a greeting: "Oh, good morning. Do you come here often?"

To his surprise both youngsters burst out laughing again.

"We come everywhere, mate," the male replied.

The female backed him up: "We come all the time, darlin'."

As if part of a double act, the male took his turn: "We're goin' now, Granddad, then we're goin' to come again, so ta-ta."

They both got to their feet and the male threw down a Coke can before putting an arm round his partner's waist and they set off back towards the church. Basil turned his head to watch them.

The female looked back over her shoulder and Basil heard her say, "He doesn't know what the 'ell we're on about, Dave."

Her insight was totally accurate because Basil had no idea what had amused them – perhaps it was something to do with the smartphone. He had never owned one, and in fact he was almost completely ignorant where modern technology was concerned. He looked at his ancient wristwatch and was happy that the pub was about to open.

Back at the care home Sami was very grateful that Imran could help him load the car. The plastic was not very pliable and it took the two of them twenty minutes to press it into the estate car's boot.

"Shall I come with you to The Tip, Sami?"

"No, no, Imran. I'm sure Matron will need you to help out in the kitchen. I'll be fine – there's bound to be someone at The Tip to help me unload."

Sami arrived at The Tip two minutes later and joined a queue of vehicles waiting to deposit their garbage. It was his first visit and when he finally entered the main area he wondered where to park; he looked around for guidance, but all the staff were engaged so he pulled up next to the bottle bank and got out.

"'Ere, you, don't park there mate. No one can get to the bottle bank."

It was Sami's first meeting with Fred Urmston.

"Where would you like me to park, then, sir?"

"There's a space down by the plastic-bottle bin. What have you brought, anyway?"

"Some large sheets of plastic covering."

"Right, that's residual waste. Take it to that large container down on the left; my colleague will take a look at it for you."

Sami followed Fred Urmston's instructions; he opened the car boot and started to pull out the plastic sheets.

"What 'ave you got there, mate?" This time it was Jack Sugden asking the question from the top of the residual-waste ramp.

"Your colleague has directed me here, sir, with this plastic."

Fred Sugden descended and joined Sami by his vehicle.

"Blimey, mate, have you just had twelve new settees?"

"No, actually, sir, they're from some new mattresses."

"Do you live in a mansion, then?"

"No, no, just a place in Town End; I decided to replace all our mattresses at the same time, you see."

"You could have brought the old mattresses here, mate."

"Really? I'll remember that next time, sir."

"In about twenty years, eh? Mind you, I'll be retired then."

Sami smiled and got back into the car. As he was about to drive off he noticed, through his rear-view mirror, a member of staff removing what looked like a microwave oven from the small-electrical-items container. The person left it at the top of the ramp.

CHAPTER 2

Most residents of the Town End Care Home had a snooze after lunch; Basil Weston didn't join them. The weather had perked up and it was warm for the time of year. Basil approached the staff member at the reception desk.

"Mrs Davies, I'm going to take a stroll into town – Dr Priest said I should take daily exercise."

Val Davies looked up from the computer screen: "Right-ho, Mr Weston. Now, remember to sign out and don't do anything naughty out there."

"I'll try not to, Mrs Davies, but we older chaps still have a little left, you know."

Val smiled at him while wishing that her sixty-year-old husband, Maurice, had something left.

Basil made his way to his favourite bench on Church Terrace. This time it was vacant. He sat down and reached into his jacket pocket to retrieve his packet of cigarettes; while he was fumbling around he became aware that someone had sat down on the nearby bench. He looked up and turned his head with an unlit cigarette between his lips. Immediately he recognised the young woman he had seen earlier in the day; this time she was alone and she wasn't the happy joker she had been previously. She glanced over to where Basil was sitting.

He took the initiative: "Why, hello. You've come again, I see."

The young woman adopted a serious manner. "I'm sorry about earlier."

"About what?" Basil asked.

"About us taking the . . . being silly."

"That's OK – I was young once, you know."

She managed a wan smile.

"Where's your friend this afternoon?" Basil asked.

"Oh, he's crashed out – I mean asleep."

"I see. Now I'm off to The Red Cat. Do you fancy a drink?"

"What's The Red Cat?"

"Oh, sorry – it's the local pub; it's actually The Red Lion, but everyone round here calls it The Red Cat."

She smiled again, this time with some warmth. "No, thanks, I've got to wait for Dave."

"He's going to come, then, is he?"

She smiled again while thinking to herself, 'not with all the junk he's had today'.

She attempted to change the subject: "Are you married?"

Basil looked down before answering: "I was, but my wife died a few months ago."

The young woman looked genuinely sympathetic. "Oh, I am sorry."

Basil took a deep breath. "Well, actually, it was a bit of a relief – she had aggressive breast cancer, you see."

The young woman did not want to delve any further into this part of the old man's life.

"Have you got any kids?" she asked.

"No, we did try, but none came along. How about you? Have you got any brothers and sisters?"

"Yeah, I've got two half-sisters, but I haven't seen them for years. I was fostered out when I was five and later I lived in a council home."

Basil could sympathise: "I live in a home these days. It's not bad really – you see, I couldn't manage when June died. Are you living locally?"

"Yes, we're guarding Dave's grandma's place – she's away for a time."

She added no more because Dave was now approaching; she stood up and went to meet him.

"Goodbye," Basil called after her.

She remained silent, however.

He watched as the couple met up, and noticed that the young

man was concerned about something because he became quite animated while looking over his partner's shoulder directly at Basil. After a few seconds though he turned to face the same direction as his partner; Basil noticed his hand on her back as though guiding her away.

Basil would have been enlightened if he had heard Dave's interactions. The young man wanted to know what his partner, Stacie, had discussed with him.

"What did that old fart want from you, Stacie?"

"Nothing really, Dave. I was just passing the time of day."

"Well, I hope that's all it was, Stacie. You didn't tell him our address, did you?"

"No, of course I bloody didn't – I'm not stupid."

This assessment seemed to calm her partner.

"I've had a text from Denny: he's bringing the car up here tomorrow."

"That is not a good idea, Dave – you know he always brings trouble."

"Stacie, I've told you before that he looked out for me when we were both in the young offenders' institution."

"And he's preyed on you ever since! Now look, you can't have him crashing into your life when he feels like it. What does he want this time?"

"He didn't tell me in his text, but it's probably something to do with the car."

Stacie thought of several acid comments she could make, but this time she held her tongue; secretly she hoped the police would arrest Dave on his way north.

Basil was feeling cold on the bench; he had finished his cigarette so he decided to visit his other site of refuge, The Red Lion. The pub had welcomed him many times over the years – he even used to bring his wife on special occasions. In the past the pub did a good trade, but nowadays business was poor. Syd Fawkes, the landlord, was worried about the future. He had tried various things to attract more customers – evening entertainment, televised soccer, even meals and snacks – but all without much success; fortunately he still had some regulars, like Basil, but many were aging and most were struggling financially. On this particular afternoon business was really slack, so Syd was very pleased when Basil entered the lounge bar.

"Hi, Basil. How are you today?"

"Pretty bored to tell you the truth, Syd. It's OK being in the care home, but there's not much fun to be had. I come out as often as possible because I can't have a smoke in there and alcohol is off limits as well. How's business, by the way?"

"Not good, Basil. The lease runs out quite soon and I don't think I'll attempt to renew it. By the way, you old devil, I've seen you chatting up a young lass a couple of times recently."

"Well, Syd, we mature chaps have all the chat-up lines; actually, I don't think she can resist me."

Basil meant his remark as a joke and he was surprised when the landlord became serious: "Look, Basil, I know that this is none of my business really, but be careful because I hear she's shacked up with some tearaway in Freda Willian's place out at the end of Brookhouse Close."

"Well, thanks for that, Syd, but I've only had a couple of chats with her; she's OK, but the lad is really objectionable. Anyway, squirt me a pint of best bitter, please."

Staff at the town tip were experiencing one of their frequent idle periods. On the whole Jack Sugden was happy with his latest recruits: they were both polite, they had turned up on time so far and the Romanian was keen to learn about recycling.

"Do you have much recycling in your country, Dimi?" Jack had asked one day.

"No, not really, Mr Sugden. I want to learn as much as I can about the British system so that when I return home I can perhaps start up my own business. Winston and I have Wi-Fi at our hostel, so each evening I'm doing research into waste collection."

"Wow, that must be really exciting for you, Dimi! What does Winston research?"

"Dating websites mainly."

"Has he had any luck? I can see his selling blurb now: handsome rubbish collector from South London seeks partner with limited sense of smell."

The office phone brought the conversation to a close. Mollie

Knowles took the call and Jack was surprised when she started to take notes while the call was still in progress. Finally, after two minutes or so, she replaced the receiver.

"What was all that about, Mollie?" Jack asked.

"That was our big boss at the town hall; he's coming to visit this site next week and he's bringing a couple of councillors and our local MP."

"Did he say why, Mollie?"

"Jack, he told me the government are working with town and rural councils to assess the effectiveness of recycling in this country." However, Mollie reckoned he knew the real reason: "They'll be after making savings, Jack, so now we need to get our act together. I need to find out when they are coming. George Rampling wouldn't be specific, Jack; he just said sometime next week, but I can ring my friend in the Environment Department. She might be able to tell us the day and time."

"Right, I bet they're trying to catch us on the hop, Mollie. Now we need to make all our staff aware."

"Shall we mention the cost-cutting, Jack?"

"Yep, might as well. I don't want to keep anyone in the dark – I'll ask them all to call in at the end of today's shift."

Dave Pringle had asked his grandmother if he could stay in her bungalow while she was on holiday for a specific reason: he had fallen out big time with two former friends over a drugs deal. He had no doubt that Jed Wrench and Billy Albright would be searching for him, so he needed to stay hidden, but the trouble was he was running short of cash.

When he and Stacie returned to the property on this particular afternoon he outlined the problem to her: "Look, darlin', we need dosh urgently. Have you got any ideas?"

Stacie thought for a moment.

"Well, you know that old guy we took the mick out of earlier? He lives in a care home and I bet there are several pensioners living there who are quite well off."

"So what are you suggesting, then?"

"Look, I'll try and make friends with the old guy so I can find out who's got expensive items, then perhaps we can get in and nick a few things – I mean, some of the old farts may not miss things for some time."

Dave gave the idea some thought, and for once he did not poo-poo Stacie's opinion.

"OK, so how do you go about getting close to the guy?"

"He seems to sit on that bench at the same time every day for a smoke; I'll make sure I'm there tomorrow – not with you, of course. I'll get chatting and offer to visit him in the care home so I can have a look round. I bet he's quite lonely now his wife his dead."

"OK, Stacie, it's worth a try."

Dave would have added more, but he was interrupted by the sound of a car's engine. Both he and Stacie rushed to the window; a BMW was on the drive. The engine stopped and a short, rotund person got out – Denny Mace had arrived.

"Oh, God, Dave, look who it is! Let's get rid of him asap."

Dave went and opened the kitchen door.

"In 'ere, Denny."

"I had a hell of a time finding you, Dave; even the bloody satnav was confused. Actually, it's a good job you are 'ere – there's 'alf of Brixton trying to find you back in the Smoke."

"You 'aven't told anyone, 'ave you, Denny?"

"No, mate. See, I need your 'elp."

'Now, there's a surprise!' Stacie thought to herself while remaining silent.

"Is it to do with the motor, Denny?"

"It certainly is, Dave. It's a real beauty. I nicked it in Barnes; this woman left the keys in when she went to answer the phone in 'er 'ouse. Don't worry though – I've changed the number plates. I want to leave it with you out 'ere in the sticks till I can arrange a respray. Now you've got a garage 'ere, I see, so I'll put it in so it'll be perfectly safe – I mean, it must be worth twenty grand, don't you think?"

Stacie now butted in before Dave could offer his evaluation of the vehicle's worth: "Are you hoping to stay 'ere as well, Denny?"

"No, darlin', I want to get to Manchester to meet my brother; he's coming out of Strangeways Prison soon. I'll just stay 'ere tonight, then you can get me to Stoke so I can catch a choo-

choo to the lovely capital of the North."

"Do you want me to take you in the car to the railway station, Denny?"

"Not a good idea, Dave, but thanks for the offer. Is there a bus out 'ere in the Wild West?"

Stacie knew the answer: "There is, Denny. You can catch it in the High Street outside the post office."

"Right, great! I'll let you know soon when I can collect the motor. Now I'm feelin' hungry, so if there's a caff round 'ere I'll treat you both."

Dave was unsure, but Stacie had the answer: "There's The Red Lion, Denny – they do bar snacks, I believe."

"Right, darlin', let's go."

It was another quiet night at The Red Lion, so Syd Fawkes was delighted when three new customers entered. He recognised the young woman immediately and he was pretty sure he'd seen one of the men before, but the short plump male was new to him.

"Good evening, folks. Now, what can I get you?"

The unknown male took the lead: "Right, mate, we two blokes will have a pint of your best bitter." He turned to Stacie: "What will you 'ave, darlin'?"

"Sparkling water, ice and lemon, please, Denny."

Denny turned to Dave: "You're in for an exciting time tonight, mate."

"You're not from round here, are you, sir?"

"No, mate, I'm from South London. Ever been there?"

Syd smiled at him. "Only once, sir – that was enough. Now, would you like to peruse our snacks menu?"

"Yeah, mate, we're all starvin'."

"Right, you all sit down and I'll bring the drinks and the paperwork over."

Stacie led the way to a table by the main window.

When they were seated, Dave asked a question in a low voice: "Denny, is it a good idea to give out personal information?"

"Don't worry, mate – everyone up 'ere seems to be as thick as shit."

Stacie was about to protest, but the drinks had arrived.

18

Over at the town tip the permanent staff members were not happy to be called to a meeting at the end of their shift.

Jack Sugden attempted to keep things calm: "Look, lads, I won't keep you long, but you need to know that we're to have a visit from our MP and local councillors, together with the boss of the council's Environment Department."

Fred Urmston asked the questions that were in everyone's mind: "Why and when, Jack?"

Jack adopted a serious expression. "Mollie and I reckon the council is looking to save money because Her Majesty's bleeding government has cut its grant to the council, so our jobs may be on the line. Now, Mollie here has been delving and she's found out when the visit will happen. You tell them, Mollie, please."

"Right, boys, I have a friend who works at the council offices in the Environment Department; she's in a senior position, so she knows what's what. She tells me the inspection will take place in a couple of days' time at nine in the morning."

Jack had something to add: "I reckon they're coming early on a weekday in the hope that no one will be depositing their waste, so they can then report that cuts are needed. Now, what Mollie suggests is this: we all ask our families and friends to bring any rubbish they wish to get rid of when the group is here."

Mollie's suggestion received general agreement, but Dimitri asked for more information. "Mr Sugden, sir, you said an MP was coming, and I'm sorry but I don't understand."

"That's OK, Dimi. MP stands for Member of Parliament. The person we have in this constituency is the Right Honourable Tobias Argent; he's a Conservative."

Fred Urmston revealed his political beliefs directly: "He's a stupid Tory prat, Dimi, and it's about time they stuck him in the House of bleedin' Lords."

Dimitri was still not sure he understood, but he kept quiet to preserve the peace.

Jack brought the meeting to an end: "Right, lads, that's all. Now remember, do your best drumming up rubbish."

CHAPTER 3

At the care home it was Basil Weston's least favourite part of the day – dinner time was always a bore. Basil could enter the dining room unaided; most of the other residents, with the exception of Ethel Stones, needed help to come from their rooms or from the lounge. Basil always made sure he was first so he could choose his table. He liked to sit at a small table by the main window so he could watch the goings-on out in the street and avoid having to share with some inarticulate idiot. He also knew he would have to wait perhaps for half an hour to be served. This evening was worse than most, but at last, and to his surprise, the Matron appeared with his starter.

"I'm sorry you've had to wait so long, Basil, but I'm very short-staffed this evening."

"Has somebody walked off the job again, Matron?"

"No, but two staff have rung in sick."

"Do you believe them?"

"No, but I have to take their word."

"Now, what you need, Matron, is some staff on these zero-hours contracts."

"I have heard of them, Basil, and I think you're right, but I'll have to clear it with the directors, of course. Anyway, eat your soup – I'll bring the main course in a while."

Basil was sure it would be quite a while. He was not wrong, because he had to wait half an hour after finishing his tepid tomato soup before an equally cool chicken pie appeared.

However, Basil did not complain; instead he offered the Matron some advice: "Matron, I know this young couple who I meet in town sometimes; they seem to be out of work, so I could mention that this care home has vacancies, if you like."

"Please do that, Basil, but stress that any work is strictly temporary and without guaranteed hours."

Over at The Red Lion Denny, Dave and Stacie were still in situ; the men were now on their sixth pint each; Stacie, on the other hand, had stuck to sparkling water, much to male annoyance.

"Hey, darlin', surely just one gin and tonic won't knock you out."

"That's very true, Denny, but I don't want to spend all your dosh – I mean, you must have spent at least fifty quid on Dave and me so far."

"No worries, darlin'. I've just had a good week and there's the car too, of course. By the way, Dave, how are you for cash?"

"OK for the moment, Denny, but we'll need to do somethin' soon."

"Not much goin' on round 'ere, I bet, Dave."

"Well, Denny, folks round 'ere may be off the ball security-wise – it isn't like London."

"Yeah, Dave, you may right. Now, I passed a care home on my way to your place – they're often a soft touch, especially with a load of old fogies in them. Now listen – I'll go to Manchester tomorrow and I'll leave you 500 quid to pay for looking after the motor; I'll leave the keys with you too cos I know I can trust you and Stacie. I'll keep in touch – you've still got your mobile, I take it. Actually, I've got one of them smartphones."

"How did you get that, Denny? They cost two arms and a few legs."

"No trouble, Dave. See, me and my mate Anthony 'ave a system: he's got a scooter; I sit on the back as he drives it around town; now, when he spots some idiot using their phone near the kerb he drives real close and I snatch the phone – dead simple."

"Do you always grab a smartphone, then?" Stacie wanted to know. "Not always, darlin', but even the crap ones like Dave's are worth a bit. Now, can you find out if there's a paint-spray business around 'ere?"

Unbeknown to the trio, Syd Fawkes had heard most of their conversation. Business was slack again, so it was easy for him to concentrate on just three customers' voices.

Later when Dave and Stacie were alone in their bedroom Dave took up Denny's idea: "Stacie, I bet that old boy you speak to has got some valuables. He won't really need them, will he? I bet he'll be dead in the next couple of years."

"He lives in the care home, Dave, which may not be as easy to break into as Denny thinks."

"Yeah, OK, but I tell you what: when you meet him next, chat him up about the care home, but don't make it too obvious."

Stacie made no comment. She turned over in the bed and closed her eyes.

Denny left early the next morning. Stacie walked with him into town and showed him where to catch the bus into Stoke-on-Trent, from where he could take a train to Manchester.

"I'll be in touch, darlin'."

Stacie smiled at him, but made no other comment; she felt like saying, "Don't bother, darlin' – we can live perfectly well without you."

When he was safely on the bus Stacie walked towards the church because she knew that Dave would have gone back to bed to sleep off the night before. It was a warm, cloudless morning, ideal for taking the sun. Stacie sat on one of the benches on Church Terrace. She rolled up her jeans as far as possible and undid two buttons on her blouse; she sat with her legs wide apart, arms outstretched, eyes closed.

"Well, hello there. Taking the sun, are we?"

Stacie opened her eyes and looked to her left. It was the old boy again.

"Yes, I am. You know what it's like in this country – you have to make the most of the sun when it appears."

"Yes, that's right. May I join you?"

Stacie retracted her limbs, but left her blouse unbuttoned.

"Yes, please do. I'm Stacie, by the way."

Basil sat beside her, but not too close.

"I'm Basil and I'm here for a smoke – would you like one?"

"Yes please, Basil. I know fags are supposed to be bad for you, but I started smoking about ten years ago."

Basil laughed out loud. "I can beat you there, Stacie, by about sixty years. Try one of these."

Basil held out the packet; Stacie leaned over and took one.

"Thanks, Basil."

Basil lit both cigarettes and then he and Stacie inhaled in silence.

"You told me that you live in the local care home, didn't you, Basil?"

Basil exhaled and nodded.

"How do you find it?"

Basil thought for a moment before replying: "Well, I suppose it's OK, but all the other residents are less fit than I am, both physically and mentally; that's why I like to come here for a smoke."

"Do you have to live there, Basil?"

"No, not really, but when my wife died it seemed a good idea because I was pretty hopeless at looking after myself; so I sold my house, furniture and effects to raise enough money with other savings to afford the rent. I'm stuck there now, to tell you the truth."

"What about the others, Basil?"

"I don't know their full circumstances, of course, but I reckon that some, like me, are self-supporting; others are there because the local authority pays. Actually, the place needs more staff and I've suggested that the Matron advertises for people who are willing to work part-time."

"I'd be interested, Basil. Can you mention me to the Matron?"

"Actually, Stacie, I already have. Anyway, that's enough about me; now what about you? Why are you up here? I reckon, from your accent, that you're from the South."

"Dead right, Basil – I'm a Londoner, from Battersea actually."

"So why are you here in Staffordshire?"

"I've come with Dave – we're looking after his grandma's place while she's away."

"So you'll be going back to London sometime."

"Yeah, but I don't know when – that's why I could do with a job."

Basil glanced at his wristwatch. "Do you fancy a coffee, Stacie? The Red Cat is open now."

"Cheers, Basil; but hey, we'd better put these fags out."

"Dead right, Stacie. It really pisses me off that we can't have a smoke in a pub any more – it's killed the trade, and I'm worried that the one pub left in this town will close soon. I go in every day to support Syd, the landlord."

Basil rose a little unsteadily from the bench; Stacie did the same. Both of them dropped their cigarette ends on to the ground before walking off in the direction of the pub.

It was another quiet day in The Red Lion, so Syd Fawkes was delighted when Basil entered, especially as he had an extra customer with him. Syd recognised the young woman immediately. She went to occupy the same seating area as on her previous visit with the two men. Basil came over to the bar.

"I see you picked up a young bit of stuff, then, Basil?"

"Well, Syd, we older blokes have the experience, you see; we know how to treat the ladies, especially the young ones." Basil tapped the side of his nose as he gave this assessment.

"I've seen her in here before, Basil, with a couple of young guys." Syd lowered his voice. "You need to be careful, Basil – her male friends are certainly dodgy. I overheard some of their conversation – they're on the make and, what's worse, they're from South London. Now, we don't get Londoners up here for their health, do we?"

"Don't worry about Stacie, Syd – she's fine. She is from London, but she and her mates are doing an old girl a favour by looking after her property while she's away. Actually though, Stacie is looking for work up here; I'd be quite happy to see her employed at the care home, which is very short of staff."

Syd looked doubtful and changed the subject: "Right, Basil, what can I get you?"

After ordering the coffees, Basil joined Stacie.

"Syd will bring them over, Stacie."

"You had quite a chat there, Basil."

"Yes, right, I was telling Syd that you're looking for a job."

"Has he got one going here in the pub, Basil? I've done bar work before."

"No, love, he hasn't, but the care home will probably advertise for staff in the very near future."

"Can you put a word in for me, Basil, so I'm at the front of the queue?"

"Of course I will, Stacie – no problem."

CHAPTER 4

Mollie Knowles and Jack Sugden had taken considerable pains to prepare thoroughly for the official inspection visit. Mollie had found out from her friend in the council's Environment Department that Tobias Argent, MP, had insisted the inspection team arrive close to opening time on the scheduled day; she also warned Mollie that the real reason for the visit was to seek evidence with a view to saving money, probably by making redundancies. Mollie guessed that the one local councillor in the party would be more sympathetic to the workers. Bill Nugent had represented the local Labour Party for several years. Mollie guessed that he would be piggy in the middle and would most likely come under pressure from both right-wing politics and members of staff hoping to retain their jobs. Mollie's friend had also found out that Tobias Argent had insisted that only one local councillor should accompany him, together with Mr George Rampling, the head of the council's Environment Department.

Jack and Mollie had realised that it was most important that The Tip appeared to be busy from the moment the gate was opened and throughout the inspection visit. Mollie, whose family lived locally, had arranged that six cars, all bearing items for recycling, would be there on the dot when The Tip opened. Jack had bought a few rounds in The Red Lion for his friends so that they too would arrive shortly after opening time. Syd Fawkes had volunteered to bring empty bottles and discarded newspapers – he was keen to keep in with his customers. Fred Urmston and Pete Fenton had both managed to persuade their partners to appear with vehicles suitably charged up with items of household waste as well. Mollie and Jack had managed to persuade most of the volunteers to make several visits so that The Tip appeared to be fully occupied even on a weekday.

The official party met at the council offices. Tobias Argent was not at all happy to have to share a vehicle with a political opponent, but realised he had to maintain the air of someone dedicated to his constituency. Bill Nugent felt exactly the same about his political travelling companion, so he had taken the initiative to speak to George Rampling on the previous day to arrange his own seating position next to the driver, who happened to be George himself. This arrangement suited Tobias because he would be alone in the rear in a rather regal position. At eight thirty precisely the trio took their seats and set off for the Chelford town tip. Bill chatted to George en route while Tobias maintained a dignified silence in the rear.

The inspection team had their first surprise when George turned into the side road where The Tip entrance was situated; none of them had expected a queue at this time in the morning, but they found themselves the seventh car in the line. Tobias was not happy.

"Mr Rampling, please get out and tell the other drivers to pull over – I need to enter immediately."

George undid his safety belt, but before he could open his door all the other cars moved forward into The Tip. It was exactly nine o'clock. George followed the others for a short distance, but parked in the staff car park.

"Right, now, Mr Rampling, I want to speak to whoever is in charge straight away."

Bill Nugent realised he must become involved or be totally sidelined.

"I have visited the facility before, Mr Argent, so if you follow me I will find Jack Sugden, the supervisor, who is probably in his office."

George Rampling had no desire to be ammunition in a political spat so he made his stand: "Gentlemen, I will go and observe so I can report back to you both in due course."

Bill Nugent thanked him; Tobias Argent didn't.

"I shall carry out my own assessment, Mr Rampling, but off you go."

Jack and Mollie had observed the negotiations from the sanctuary of the office.

"Have you met either of these two blokes before, Jack?"

"Bill Nugent has been here a couple of times, Mollie, but not recently."

"Which is him, Jack?"

"He's the short guy in the red anorak, Mollie. He's a decent, normal, down-to-earth guy. I've never met our MP – he looks a right stuck-up prat. Fancy coming to a rubbish dump in a posh overcoat!"

Jack said no more because the duo was now at the threshold. Neither man would give way and it was with some difficulty that they somehow squeezed in side by side.

"Good morning, gentlemen. I am Jack Sugden, the supervisor, and this is Mrs Knowles, the administrator."

Tobias reacted first: "Yes, right, now, I am Tobias Argent, your local Member of Parliament and I'm here on government business as a member of the House of Commons Environment Committee. The observations I make here today will be reported to the committee and could well influence government policy in the very near future."

Once again Bill Nugent felt he had to establish some influence: "Hi there. You'll know me because I've visited the facility before. I'm here to ensure that any assessments are based on facts."

Tobias frowned, but did not openly oppose Bill's statement; instead he issued his modus operandi: "First I have questions for you two, then I shall interview a member of staff; I shall also speak to customers and observe how the facility works."

Both Mollie and Jack turned to Bill Nugent with questioning expressions.

Bill took the bait: "I shall be present at all times and I may answer some of Mr Argent's questions myself."

Tobias was obviously irritated by this, but pressed on: "Now, if this lady could leave us for a short time I have some questions for you, Mr Sugden."

Mollie took the hint and went to the Ladies toilet.

"How long have you worked here, Mr Sugden?"

"I started about twelve years ago; of course then I was a junior member of staff, but I've managed to rise through the ranks so that today I am the supervisor."

"Are you happy with the job, then?"

"Yes, I am, Mr Argent; I earn above the minimum wage and I'm in the local authority's pension scheme."

"You seem to be very busy today, Mr Sugden – is it typical?"

"I can honestly say that business has become more intense over the time I've been here, and today we ensure that people's garbage is more accurately classified and disposed of than it was in the recent past."

Tobias Argent looked dubious, so Bill Nugent sought to offer a more positive approach from his own questions. "So, Jack, you need several members of staff to ensure that the system works efficiently?"

"Yes, Mr Nugent, that is correct. At the moment I have three experienced staff and two recent recruits."

Tobias saw an opportunity to pursue his inquisition: "Right – I need to speak to one of these newcomers. Where are they now, please?"

"They are helping customers under supervision, Mr Argent."

"Right, go and find the nearest one so I can ask some questions. What about that tall chap over by the bottle bank?"

"He is Dimitri Rotarescu, Mr Argent."

"Dimi what? Surely he's not English."

"No, he isn't – I believe he's from Romania."

Tobias Argent adopted a stern look as he faced Jack Sugden: "Do you mean to tell me you've hired an immigrant who has come over here and taken one of our jobs?"

"Mr Argent, I've had great difficulty hiring English workers; I can assure you I have tried, but either they turn the job down or they stick it only for a week or two."

Once again Bill Nugent attempted to support Jack: "I bet he's a good worker, isn't he, Jack?"

Before Jack could answer, Tobias became decisive: "I'll see about that! Call him in immediately, please."

Jack left the Portakabin and made his way over to the bottle bank.

"Dimi, a couple of chaps want to have a chat with you."

"What about, Mr Sugden?"

"Just to see how you're getting on. They're waiting for you in the office – I'll take over from you here."

Dimitri was obviously apprehensive, but, nevertheless, he made his way to the interview.

Both politicians were impressed when Dimitri joined them in the office; he was tall, dark and smart. For once Tobias was outgunned by a socialist.

"Thanks very much for coming to speak to us, Mr Rotarescu. This is Tobias Argent, our local Member of Parliament, and I am Bill Nugent, a local councillor."

Dimi smiled down at Tobias. "Good morning, sir."

The MP had regained some sangfroid: "I need to ask you first why you came to my country?"

"Sir, I came to find work. I saved up to pay my fare and I decided to come to this area because it is much cheaper to live here than in London."

Tobias knew this to be true.

"Well, it's not much of a job, is it?"

"Sir, it is a start for me, and I can send some money back to Romania to support my family. In addition I am studying waste collection here so that, when I go back home, I can start my own business in recycling."

Tobias didn't believe him.

"How on earth can you study?"

"Sir, at the hostel where I am staying I have access to a laptop and Wi-Fi so I can find out about the management of recycling practice as set out in ISO 15270. At the moment I am researching the salvage of complex products, such as lead from car batteries and gold from circuit boards. You see, I believe there will be a market for such commodities in my country when I return there and I am very grateful to Great Britain for giving such rich learning opportunities."

Both politicians, to use a cricketing term, were stumped.

"May I return to my duties now, please?"

Bill Nugent returned to the crease: "Yes, please do – and thank you."

Tobias Argent was not happy.

"Mr Nugent, it makes me furious when some immigrant like him comes over here and shows some enterprise. Where are our young people?"

"Well, Mr Argent, perhaps there is something wrong with our education system."

"What do you mean, man?"

"Well, perhaps there is too much emphasis on testing and not enough on allowing personal development and creativity."

"I hope you are not blaming my party."

"No, I'm not – the problem has been compounded by both parties over many years. I can even remember when I was about to sit a maths exam years ago. My teacher told me I was borderline and then he said, 'Nugent, if you pass you'll never need to study maths again.' Right, who do we speak to next?"

Tobias was in no position to answer because he was still trying to process Bill Nugent's statement.

He was saved from any embarrassment because Mollie Knowles, who had overheard most of the interview, now entered the fray: "Gentlemen, would you like a cup of tea? I have a selection of leaves – some from Sri Lanka and others from Darjeeling and Assam. Unfortunately I don't have any from Yorkshire."

Bill Nugent smiled; Tobias Argent frowned, but both accepted Mollie's offer.

As he supped his tea Tobias made a decision: "Mr Nugent, I believe it's time we observed outside to find out how the operation works. I have heard many vehicles entering the site, which has surprised me."

Bill didn't admit it openly, but he too was surprised by the amount of traffic. Both men finished their tea and went to find George Rampling – it was his turn to face the ordure.

George Rampling was a very organised individual who was a stickler for accuracy. While Tobias and Bill had been interviewing staff he had been making notes and taking photographs. Like the politicians, he too was surprised by the amount of recycling material being deposited in the various marked containers on this particular day. Some of the vehicles had made several visits, often with very little rubbish. He had also noticed that more women than men were using The Tip. He couldn't fault the staff in any way – they were efficient, polite and helpful. He noticed that most of the younger females made a beeline for the tall, dark, foreign-looking staff member.

Suddenly, from somewhere behind him he heard a voice: "Do you know if this tip is always this busy?"

George turned round and faced his questioner.

"I'm not sure, Mr Argent. Perhaps we ought to ask Mr Sugden. He's over by the residual-waste container, I believe."

From his position at the top of the ramp Jack Sugden saw the inquisition approaching him. He didn't move; he let the politicians and his boss walk up the steep ramp.

With a slight gasp, George Rampling announced the group's intention: "Mr Argent and Mr Nugent have some more questions for you, Jack."

Jack forced a smile. "Fire away, gentlemen, please."

As usual, Tobias got in first: "Is it always this busy, Mr Sugden?"

"Oh yes, and as you have probably noticed we have a noticeboard close to the exit that records details of amounts recycled each week. Mrs Knowles keeps meticulous records so our customers can see that they are helping to recycle their unwanted garbage successfully."

Bill Nugent was eager to support his local community: "So you need all the staff you've got, then."

"Definitely, Mr Nugent," Jack assured him.

Bill continued his support: "I suppose it's most important that customers deposit their stuff accurately."

Jack agreed: "Oh yes, that's why I and my experienced staff supervise where items are to be deposited."

"What about the new staff, then?"

Jack smiled at Tobias. "They help with carrying, and of course they're learning all the time."

"Have you anything to add, Mr Rampling?"

"Well, Mr Nugent, my recorded observations largely back up Mr Sugden's points, although I've been surprised by how little some customers are bringing today."

"But surely that's a good thing because it shows people are acting responsibly."

As if to back up Bill Nugent's assessment the party of four watched as Dimitri carried four empty wine bottles for a smartly dressed, youngish female to the bottle bank. Tobias was about to

31

make a negative comment, but he was interrupted by the arrival of an estate car which had four mattresses perilously attached to its roof rack.

Jack leapt on the opportunity: "Now, gentlemen, you can see that we have to deal with heavy loads as well."

At this moment Tobias judged that the time was right to announce the real reason for the visit: "Right, everybody, we need now to return to the office for a more formal meeting. Mr Sugden, please ask Mrs Knowles to take notes."

It was quite a crush for them in the office – the men had to stand to allow Mollie to sit at the desk.

"Can you manage shorthand, Mrs Knowles?"

"Yes, Mr Argent, I can, and I suggest that, when this meeting has concluded, I type them up on my computer and either print them out or send them by email attachment for each of you to scrutinise. It would be easier, of course, if I had a sound-recording device."

"Excellent suggestion, Mrs Knowles," Bill said in support.

Every eye now turned to Tobias Argent, who immediately sought to set the agenda: "Now, as I'm sure you all know, local authorities have to save money whilst, at the same time, maintaining the highest standards, not only in waste management but in other important areas as well, so I ask you all for your ideas." He paused and looked from one face to another.

Bill Nugent was the first to react: "Well, Mr Argent, you have seen for yourself a very efficient system here today, so I believe things should remain as they are."

Jack and George Rampling both nodded their agreement.

"Out of the question, gentlemen! There must be savings."

Bill Nugent was slow to anger, but he realised what the MP's ploy was.

"Well, I've no doubt your party will suggest privatisation, won't it?"

"Not necessarily, Mr Nugent, but it's a possibility."

"More than that, surely, because your party is experienced in weakening local authorities financially before criticising them for falling standards and then forcing privatisation. It happens in the education world all the time."

Tobias Argent did not enjoy being rumbled by a Labour councillor.

"The status quo must change, and all I'm doing is seeking your ideas. I mean, perhaps you could charge a small entrance fee for people to use the facility."

"May I remind you, Mr Argent, that this facility is partly self-financing because some of the waste deposited here can be sold on. Not all of it goes into landfill."

Bill Nugent's information caused Tobias to pause.

Bill took the opportunity to express more of his party's views: "We in Labour know what your party is about, and that is privatisation. I feel quite sure that when you report back to the parliamentary committee you and your Tory colleagues will recommend that waste disposal is taken over by the private sector."

"That is not the case, Mr Nugent; what my party is seeking is value for money. I'm sure that this facility, for example, is overstaffed. Why does it need both a supervisor and an administrator, for instance?"

Mollie Knowles had heard enough. She held out her pad and Biro to Tobias Argent.

"Here you are, sir. Please take shorthand notes; I will leave."

Jack took Mollie's lead: "Perhaps, sir, you, with your great knowledge of rubbish, should decide which is residual waste and which can be reused."

Tobias was outnumbered but defiant; he turned to Bill Nugent: "Remember this: when your party ran the country years ago, it was dominated by the trade unions and the national finances got into one hell of a state. The only way to run a positive national economy is to work efficiently so that money is not wasted. The systems at this facility need to change, and I shall recommend that staffing is cut. Now you must excuse me – I have an important meeting to attend."

Tobias turned and attempted to squeeze past the other two men.

"When I've typed up my notes where shall I send them, sir?"

Mollie received no reply because Tobias Argent had now left the Portakabin."

Fred Urmston and Pete Fenton had developed their own system over the years. Pete always helped people who were depositing small electrical items, like microwave ovens. He took them off people at the top of the ramp and told them he would place them in the waste container for them. Most people were very grateful and it was rare for them to insist that they deposit the items themselves. Pete waited till they had returned to their vehicle before scrutinising the unwanted item thoroughly. If he judged the item might be still in working order he retained it at the top of the ramp. At the end of the working day he and Fred would wait till Jack was in the toilet or the Portakabin before sneaking the item to Fred's old estate car, and when they were sure no one was looking they would stick the item in the boot. Later on, in Fred's garage, they would decide if the thing was saleable. Their initiative often added a useful sum to their wages. If the item was beyond repair they took it back to The Tip the next day.

Today the inspection meeting had given them an ideal opportunity to cash in. Pete had collared two microwave ovens and an old record player – all seemed to be in reasonable condition. They were moving them to Fred's car when they met an unforeseen snag. Winston Green, the new recruit, offered to help carry one of the items.

"No, mate, we're OK – they're not 'eavy."

Winston was not put off by Fred's assessment.

"What are you going to do with them, man?"

"This time Pete tried to put him off: "Well, mate, some of the better electrical things need a further expert assessment so they can be recycled in the best possible way; we'll take them to the expert tonight."

"Who is this expert, then?"

Fred took up the burden: "No one you would know, mate."

Even this did not put off their interrogator.

"If they're any good there might be money in it for us, eh?"

"Now, that's against the rules."

Fred offered no more information after he had said this because he was saved by his MP, who was leaving the Portakabin.

"Come on, Pete," he said, "time to shut up shop."

He closed the boot, then he and Pete went back to their duties, leaving a somewhat bemused Winston.

In the Portakabin things had become sombre.

"What will happen, do you think, chaps?" Mollie posed the question.

Bill answered her: "I have no doubt that Argent wants to see this facility privatised or closed down. All this parliamentary business is a bluff – the decision will already have been made."

"But what will folks do with their excess rubbish?" This time it was Jack asking the question.

Bill believed he had the answer: "The Tories will encourage private firms to take it – at a price, of course."

George Rampling had been silent up to this point, but now he interjected, "All that will mean is that people will dump their rubbish in the countryside – quite a few do it already."

Bill agreed, but added a different twist: "What you say is true, Mr Rampling, but some so-called firms will take people's cast-offs at a price and then dump them."

"Shall I warn my staff, Bill, that their jobs are at risk?"

"In my experience, Jack, bosses can choose one of three options to deal with probable closure: one is to ignore it and say nothing, a second is to drip-feed the bad news and the third is to admit closure will take place in the near future."

"Which is best in your view?"

"Each has its problems, Jack. Staff get very annoyed if their boss is thought to have kept the bad news totally secret. With the third method they tend to look for a new job straight away, which is understandable but causes turmoil in the short term."

"So you would recommend the drip-feed method, then, Bill?"

"On balance, yes, but even this method has its downside: staff start asking questions, so the drip feed has to be very carefully thought out if staff members are to be retained."

Jack, George and Mollie were now feeling depressed.

Bill Nugent made an attempt to lighten their mood: "I can foresee that in the future all public services will be privatised. Just imagine a testicle-removal service run by a major supermarket – of course, customers would need access to a national appeal service. Offbollock might be a suitable title."

His trio audience managed faint smiles before Mollie summed up their thoughts: "Perhaps Bollock Off would be better, Mr Nugent."

CHAPTER 5

Staff at the Town End Care Home had requested an urgent meeting with the Matron. June Bailey had guessed what their problem was because she knew many were overworked and often ordered to undertake tasks for which they had had no training; she had therefore taken the initiative to ease problems before the meeting took place: she had advertised for temporary staff in the local newspapers. So far, unfortunately, no one had applied; nevertheless she could approach the meeting with some positive news.

June had decided when the meeting should take place – she had told all permanent staff to be in her office at 10.30 a.m. because by then all the residents would have had breakfast and staff would have catered for their special needs before they took a break for morning coffee, which was timed for eleven o'clock. The main advantage for June was the fact that the meeting could only last thirty minutes – enough time for her to prevent any major mutiny. All staff members appeared on time in June's office. June, herself, was not there to meet them because she knew, from her extensive experience, that it was better for her to make a late entrance with information aimed to catch the moaners off guard.

At ten thirty-four June strode into her crowded office.

"Good morning, everyone. Sorry to have kept you waiting. Now, I believe I have some good news for you: the directors have agreed that we need more support staff and I have already placed adverts in the local newspaper and on the noticeboard in our local supermarket."

June's opening attack worked for a few seconds before Maggie

Reeder, the cook, asked the pertinent question "Has anyone applied yet, Matron?"

"Well, Ms Reeder, it's early days, of course, but I have no doubt that we will have applications very shortly."

June looked around her staff; it was clear that not one of them was completely satisfied.

Val Davies, the secretary, voiced what they were all feeling: "Things can't go on like this, Matron – we're all exhausted. You need to employ more staff or we will all look elsewhere for employment."

June was forced to use another of her leadership ploys: she asked them all a question. "Well, do any of you have suggestions to attract more staff?"

She did not expect any ideas and was surprised when Sami Barroti offered two: "Matron, you could ask us all here to approach our families and friends to see if any fancy working here."

Maggie Reeder reacted before June: "Now look, I don't want some untrained idiot in my kitchen, thank you."

At this point June managed to interject, "I totally agree, Ms Reeder. Now, what the directors have agreed to is this: we appoint workers on zero-hours contracts to fill unskilled jobs on a temporary basis. Mrs Davies here will make a record of suitable personnel who can be called in when we are under most pressure – I am thinking mainly of cleaners and laundry workers, of course."

"Do you really think, Matron, that there are people out there willing to work on that basis?"

"Yes, without doubt, Ms Reeder – students, for instance, or young mothers whose children are at school, or even pensioners seeking to boost their earnings. Many firms these days offer this type of employment."

Despite this reassurance June could see that no one was really convinced.

She turned to Sami: "What was your second idea, Sami?"

"Well, Matron, I thought that some of our residents might know of people who may be looking for part-time work."

Sami's idea brought instant condemnation, forcibly expressed by Maggie Reeder: "Most of our residents are totally muddled – perhaps you haven't noticed, Sami."

June decided to support her colleague: "That is not completely true, Ms Reeder; there are Basil Weston and Ethel Stones, for instance. Both are compos mentis. Now I must close this meeting because it is almost time for the residents' elevenses."

The staff would not let her off so lightly – this time Joan Setters, who had remained silent up to this point, gave a short, pithy assessment of everyone's work: "We deal every day with old people who are confused and often aggressive; most have physical disabilities as well – we must have more support urgently."

Joan's remarks met with general agreement.

June was not to be crushed, however: "I know what you are saying is true, Mrs Setters, but we must all surely remember that, despite the problems we face, our residents' difficulties mean we have employment. We need them; they need us. Now, if you can't stand the work, leave and let's hope you can find other employment in this area."

June's point was well made and she left the office on a high – for the moment, at least.

Basil Weston was sitting in the care home's lounge while the meeting was taking place. The only other resident capable of joining him without assistance was Ethel Stones; she had entered the lounge about ten minutes after him. Basil and Ethel did not get on, so when she arrived she made sure she sat well away from him. Basil did not acknowledge her presence, but continued to read the local newspaper which the town's newsagent delivered to the care home every week. On the penultimate page Basil read the advert for staff. He was interrupted, however, before he finished his scrutiny because Sami Barroti had entered the lounge. Basil put the paper down.

"How did the meeting go, Sami?"

"Not too well, Basil. As you know, we're overworked and the powers that be don't seem to be taking effective steps to improve things."

"I've just seen the advert for staff in this week's *Observer*, Sami."

"That's had no effect so far, Basil, and I doubt it will in the future. I mean, who wants to be on a zero-hours contract, just sitting around waiting for the phone to ring?"

"I know a young lass who could be interested, Sami."

"Really? Who is she?"

"Her name's Stacie – I see her sometimes in town and we've had a few chats. Now, look, I'm going for a stroll after coffee, and if I meet her I'll tell her about the job."

"Well, Basil, if you meet her, try to bring her to see Matron straight away."

"Right, Sami, I'll do that."

They were joined by Imran. Basil knew why he had come to the lounge at this time.

"The cricket's on soon, isn't it, Imran?"

"Yes, Basil, it's the first Test match – Pakistan versus England."

"You don't have a chance, Imran. Now I'm going for a stroll, and by the time I'm back I bet England will be on top, either batting or fielding."

"How much do you bet, Basil?"

Basil laughed out loud, but made no commitment. Instead he left the lounge – it was time for a smoke."

Denny Mace's generous donation of £500 was shrinking rapidly. Dave Pringle liked a drink, and neither he nor Stacie was exactly good at financial management.

"Look, Stacie, we've only got ninety-five quid left; we need a plan. What about this care home where your old mate lives?"

"He's not my mate, Dave, but I'll nip into town now and see if he's around."

"We need to get into that care home, Stacie – I bet there's loads of loot lying around. Denny will be back soon – he's good at selling stuff on. I mean, those old sods don't need stuff, do they? Many of 'em will be dead soon."

Stacie made no comment, but went to find her coat.

"See you in a bit, Dave."

"I'll come with you."

"No, you won't – the old boy doesn't like you. Just leave him to me."

Dave frowned, but said no more; instead he decided to follow Stacie at a safe distance just to see if the meeting happened.

Stacie found Basil sitting on his favourite bench. He had a lighted cigarette in his mouth.

"Hi there. Have you got one of those spare?"

Basil smiled at his new friend. "Here you are dear – I've got five left."

"Thanks. How are you today?"

"Fine, thanks. I've come out a bit early because there's cricket on later – England versus Pakistan."

Stacie had little knowledge of the game, but she simulated some interest: "Who do you reckon will win?"

"It'll be very tight, love. Oh, by the way, the care home needs more staff – there's an advert in the local paper."

Stacie now had genuine interest.

"When do the jobs start and how do I apply?"

"They need staff right now, so, I'll tell you what, let's finish our fags and I'll take you along to meet the Matron."

"Thanks – that's great. But will I be OK dressed like this?"

"Of course you will; I've heard that the situation's desperate."

Basil stood up, threw his cigarette to the ground and stubbed it out with his foot. Stacie took the hint: she stood as well, but stubbed her fag on the wooden arm of the bench.

"Right, Stacie, when we enter the care home we need to go to the reception desk to sign in. I'll ask Val Davies, the secretary, if Matron is free to see you."

"How do I address her, Basil? Do I use her name or just her title?"

"She likes everyone to acknowledge her status, Stacie, so just call her Matron."

It was only a short walk to the residence. When they got there Basil opened the door and ushered Stacie in first. She glanced round the reception area. It had certainly seen better days – the decor was gloomy and the settle by the side of the reception desk was distinctly old-fashioned. Basil strode to the desk, behind which Val Davies was looking quizzically in their direction.

Basil took the initiative: "Good morning, Mrs Davies. This is Stacie. She's looking for a job, so is Matron available, please?"

"She's in with Dr Priest at the moment, Mr Weston, but I'll go and ask. I suggest you and the young lady wait in the lounge, but sign in first, please."

Stacie had never visited a care home before and her doubts increased when she followed Basil into the lounge. Every chair was occupied by an elderly, clearly infirm person, of whom only two were male; most appeared to be either asleep or gazing vacantly into space. The scene reminded Stacie of a horror film she had seen years ago. Suddenly one of the elderly women looked up and made eye contact.

"You, girl, fetch me a cup of tea."

Basil attempted to protect his protégé: "This young lady does not work here, Miss Stones; she is a visitor."

Any further problems receded when Val Davies joined them.

"Matron can interview the young lady now – come this way, please."

Stacie's relief was now overtaken by nerves. She had never experienced a formal interview.

Basil smiled at her. "Good luck, Stacie. I'll stay here; come back after your chat with Matron and tell me how you got on."

Val Davies knocked on Matron's office door and immediately she and Stacie heard an instruction to enter. Val went in first.

"This is Stacie, Matron. She would like a job here."

"Thank you, Mrs Davies – you can leave us now."

As Val made her exit June Bailey had the opportunity to look the potential recruit up and down. She saw before her an unimpressive young person dressed in cheap clothing; she was slight of figure and her skin was sallow.

"Take a seat, please."

Stacie looked round and noticed a chair on the back wall.

"Bring it over to the desk."

Stacie followed the Matron's instruction while June Bailey went to sit behind her desk – a large, impressive piece of furniture.

"Now, I understand you would like a job here."

"Er, yes, please."

"Well, I'd better start by asking your full name."

"Stacie Holt."

"How old are you, Stacie?"

"Nineteen, Matron."

"Have you had a job before?"

"Yes, I was a part-time barmaid at the The Laughing Toad in Peckham."

"For how long, Stacie?"

"Three months, but then I came up 'ere with my partner."

"Does he or she have a job?"

"In a way, Matron – see, we're both looking after his grandma's bungalow while she's away."

"And you would like to gain separate employment?"

"Yes."

"Now, what I have to offer is work on a zero-hours contract. Do you understand what that means?"

"Sort of part-time, isn't it?"

"In a way, yes, but without specific settled hours."

"So how much would I earn, then, Matron?"

"The amount would vary from week to week, Stacie, but while you are working here you would receive the national minimum wage."

"So what would my job be?"

"Your tasks would vary – sometimes helping out in the kitchen, sometimes cleaning – but all would be pretty menial. You would not require any specific training. Now, are you still interested?"

"Yes."

"Right – good. Now there are two more things I need to clear up. Can I contact you by phone or text?"

"Yes. My partner, Dave, has a mobile and there is a landline in the bungalow."

"Good. Now, secondly, do you have transport so you can get here possibly in the evening?"

"No, but I can walk here because the bungalow is in Brookhouse Close."

"I see. Well, that's not too far away. Now, I suggest you come here tomorrow at nine o'clock and you can see the jobs that you will be required to do. Can you manage that?"

"Yes, but will I be paid?"

"For two hours, Stacie."

"Can it be cash in hand? I haven't got a bank account, see?"

"Certainly, Stacie. Now you must excuse me. I'll see you tomorrow."

Stacie left the office and almost forgot to return to the lounge, where Basil was waiting. Fortunately the lounge door was open.

"How did you get on, Stacie?"

"I got the job, Basil."

"Well done."

Stacie left the care home and walked quickly back to the bungalow. For once she had a spring in her step because someone had offered her a job, which she'd got on her own merit. She couldn't wait to tell Dave.

"Where the bloody 'ell 'ave you been, Stacie?" Dave's greeting was decidedly aggressive when she found him sitting in the bungalow's lounge.

"I got a job, Dave, at the care home."

"Doin' what?"

"Various things – and remember what Denny said."

"What did 'e say?"

"He said that care homes are often a soft touch, didn't he?"

Vaguely, through a mist of drugs and alcohol, Dave Pringle remembered the conversation. He became less aggressive.

"When do you start, then, Stacie?"

"I'm in there tomorrow at nine in the morning – the boss is going to pay me in cash."

Things were looking up.

Dave sought more information: "So what are your hours, then?"

"I'm on a special contract, Dave – it varies from week to week."

"So what do you 'ave to do – wipe old biddies' arses?"

"No, nothin' like that. They have special staff for that. I'll be 'elping in the laundry and doin' cleaning – things like that."

By now Dave was very interested: "So you'll get into the old bleeders' rooms?"

"Yeah, no doubt, Dave."

"So you can find out if any of them has got some valuables?"

"That's right, Dave."

"If they offer you any night work, take it, Stacie, because you could let me in."

"OK, Dave."

CHAPTER 6

Jack Sugden and his colleague Mollie Knowles had spent the previous night separately pondering the same problem: how to drip-feed essential information to the team at The Tip. Both knew that Fred Urmston and Pete Fenton would be asking questions as soon as they arrived for work. Fortunately Jack and Mollie arrived at the site before the other workers – with the exception of Dimitri Rotarescu, who was waiting for them by the main gate. Dimi went to check the containers while Mollie and Jack went to the office.

"Jack, I've been thinking."

"Me too, Mollie – about what to tell the workers."

"I've been thinking about that too, Jack."

"What do you reckon, Mollie?"

"Well, Jack, I believe it's important that they get the same message."

"Yeah, but what message today, Mollie?"

"Well, how about this? We call them all into the office before we open up and tell them that the powers that be are providing important data to the government."

"OK, Mollie, but then they'll ask why, won't they?"

"Global warming, Jack – it's all the rage at the moment."

"So we say that all tips in the country are having similar visits so there is nothing to worry about."

"Yes, but we'd better just add the phrase 'at the moment'."

"Why, Mollie?"

"Because in the near future we may have to drip-feed some more worrying information."

"Right you are, Mollie, but you tell them – you'll make a better job of it than me."

Mollie and Jack's anticipated problem proved to be valid because as soon as Fred Urmston and Pete Fenton arrived for work they came to the office.

Mollie was prepared for them: "I know what you're going to ask about, boys."

"We're worried about the future, Mollie, so how did the meeting go?"

"Well, Fred, I don't think we've got any immediate problem. I took notes and it's clear central government is concerned about global warming. MPs, like Tobias Argent, are probably seeking information about recycling tips across the country so that accurate data can inform government thinking and action. That's right, isn't it, Jack?"

Jack Sugden was slow to back Mollie up because he was still admiring her creative explanation. Finally he managed "Yes, that's right, Mollie. Now, lads, it's time for work. Has anybody seen Winston Green yet?"

No one had – he was late, and the one thing Jack could not stand was lateness.

"I want a word with him when he finally turns up."

"You can ask Dimi, Jack – he lives in the same hostel as Winston."

"Thank you, Mollie. Fred, ask what's-his-name to come to the office, will you?"

"Right-ho, boss."

Dimitri entered the office with a worried look on his face.

"Have I done something wrong, Mr Sugden, sir?"

"No, no, I just want to ask where your friend is – you know, what's-his-name."

Dimitri's face muscles relaxed. "If you mean Winston, I haven't seen him to talk to since dinner time yesterday; I did see him leave the hostel at about eight o'clock though."

"I'm asking because it is most important that staff arrive on time – we are being observed, you see."

Jack was interrupted by Mollie: "Winston's arrived, Jack – I've just seen him through the window."

"Right, I need a word." Jack said this as he left the Portakabin, Dimitri followed.

Jack found Winston in heated conversation with Fred and Pete. "Here – I need a word with you, son."

Winston knew what the word would be, so he got his apology in first: "Sorry, Mr Sugden – I overslept. It won't happen again."

"If it does, son, you're on your tricycle – get me?"

Winston nodded.

Pete attempted to lower the tension: "We had a tricycle brought in yesterday, Jack, but Winston might be a bit big for it."

Everyone smiled; recycling returned to normal for the moment.

Winston waited till his lunch break before he approached Fred Urmston.

"I was in touch with a couple of mates last night, Fred, and I told them about all the waste metal we deal with. They'd be interested in taking some of it off our hands – they'd pay us, of course."

"No, mate. Me and Pete rely on flogging small electrical items for a little extra."

"You misunderstand me, Fred – my mates would want fridges, washing machines . . . big items."

"Oh, so they turn up 'ere with a lorry, do they, and take what they want? Get real, man!"

"Look, I know they'd have to do it on the sly, at night."

"Winston, the place is locked up at night."

"But you could get a key – you open up sometimes, don't you?"

This was true so Fred sought further information: "How much cash are we talking about here?"

"Well, I spoke to my mate in London last night and described some of the larger metal items. The Count – he's one of my mates – said he would pay 500 quid for a lorry-load."

Fred was confused. "Is your mate from the upper classes, then?"

"No, we only call him the Count because he makes a lot of dosh. He counts it often, see."

"So how would we work it?"

"We move some fridges, etc., behind that shipping container when Jack isn't lookin'; I contact the Count; he drives up here with the readies; we let him in and help him load; then he drives off back to the Smoke to sell it on. Simple, isn't it?"

46

"What about Pete?"

"Up to you, Fred – he'd come in handy with the loading. And remember, this plan doesn't interfere with your own little fiddle."

Winston could now see that Jack was definitely interested.

"OK, Winston, I'll discuss it with Pete, but what about Dimi?"

"We leave him out, Fred – we can't have foreigners taking all our readies, can we?"

"Certainly not, Winston."

Staff at The Tip were not the only ones seeking to alter things; Tobias Argent was also determined to bring changes in line with his political creed. He had been surprised by the number of persons bringing unwanted items to The Tip during his early morning visit. He hadn't been a Member of Parliament for twenty years without developing an unhealthy cynicism. Today he had arranged to meet a faithful member of his party at The Red Lion so he could work out a way of gaining accurate data about business at The Tip.

Samantha Fagan was young, ugly and determined to be involved in politics. She had decided on the Conservative Party because the Conservatives were strongest in this rural constituency; she attended all the Young Conservatives meetings and was in the forefront when any volunteers were required. Her father, a staunch Labour supporter over many years, was disgusted with her decision, but, as Samantha often pointed out to him, his political allegiance had got him nowhere. She was therefore delighted to be invited to a meeting with the constituency MP. She did wonder why Tobias had chosen to meet in The Red Lion rather than the Conservative Club, but had no doubt that he had some important reason for his decision.

Samantha entered The Red Lion at the agreed time; there was no sign of Tobias.

"Can I get you something, dear?"

Samantha did not enjoy being linked to any form of wildlife, but maintained her composure before answering Syd Fawkes' question: "No, thank you, barman. I've arranged to meet a friend here."

"He's in the snug, darling, and he's asked me to let you in but no one else."

This information did much to settle Samantha's sense of self-worth.

"Where is the meeting place, please?"

"It's next to the toilets – you can't miss it, darling."

Samantha followed the 'Toilets' sign into a dingy passage, at the end of which was a closed door with a printed notice that said 'The Snug'. She knocked and entered. Seated before her at a table she recognised Tobias Argent, who did not get up to greet her.

"Ah, there you are."

"Not late, I hope, Mr Argent."

"No, no, certainly not, and in this private situation you can call me Tobias."

Samantha made her way to the table and sat down opposite the MP.

"I was pleased to receive your call, Tobias. Now, how can I help?"

He didn't reply immediately because someone knocked on the door and entered.

"Can I get you some drinks?"

"No, thank you, barman. And if you remember, I asked not to be interrupted so please leave us."

"Right, sir."

"Now, as I was about to say, Samantha, I would welcome your help in gathering some very important data."

"I am always keen to help the party, Tobias, so what do I need to do?"

"This local authority needs to save money so the government can take the credit for lowering the community charge."

"I understand that, Tobias."

"Good. Now, the local tip in this town is not efficient – I went there earlier this week. They've got far too many staff: there's a supervisor, a receptionist and four workers, of whom one is foreign."

"Goodness, Tobias!"

"I can see you're shocked, Samantha. Now, when I was there, after they had just opened, business was brisk – so brisk that I think they had found out about my monitoring visit. So I would like you to observe the place surreptitiously from time to time. Can you do that for me?"

"Yes, certainly."

"Good, but don't tell a soul what you're up to. I chose this place for our meeting because of this room – you see, at the local Conservative Club we might have been overheard and the last thing I want is for word of what I am doing to get out. I want accurate data with recorded dates, times and numbers of visitors so I can present hard facts. We need either for the private sector to take over The Tip or to have it closed down, as I am sure you will appreciate. Now, can you meet me here in a week's time?"

"Yes, Tobias, and I'll have the data you require."

"Good girl! And now I must go."

Tobias stood up and left the room with Samantha in tandem. They had to exit via the bar, in which Samantha noticed a pensioner chatting to a girl.

"Goodbye, both," Syd called after them.

Neither Tory acknowledged him, but nor did they know that Syd had recorded their conversation in the snug.

"Who was that bloke, Syd?"

"That Basil was our famous MP, the one and only Tobias Argent."

"Was that his bit of stuff?"

"Could be."

"Did they have a drink?" This time it was Stacie asking the question.

"No, darlin', they bloody didn't."

"What was it all about, then, Syd?"

"I'll know that when I play back the tape, Basil. In the past, when I had more customers, I used it to monitor what was going on in the snug so I could offer more drinks at the right moment."

"You should join MI5, Syd."

"Good idea, Basil – there's bound to be more cash in it than here."

Syd left his post and went to check on the snug; perhaps the MP had left something for him – a tip, for instance. Basil and Stacie stayed in the bar.

"Thanks for buying me a drink, Stacie."

"Well, it's about time I did because you've bought me several, not to mention the cigarettes. Actually I was in the care home earlier."

"I didn't see you."

"No, because I was shown the areas where I will work when required. I went to the kitchen and the laundry and met the people in charge. The cook looks like a right tyrant – I hope I don't have to work under her."

"Did Matron show you any of the residents' rooms, Stacie?"

"No, but I would like to know what they are like in case I have to clean them in the future."

"I can help you there, Stacie, because I'm allowed visitors, so why not come with me now?"

"Are you sure it will be OK, Basil?"

"Yes – no problem. I'll just have to sign you in at reception."

Syd had returned to the bar, so Stacie took back her and Basil's glasses before following her new friend to the exit.

They soon arrived at the care home.

"Stacie has come to visit me, Mrs Davies."

The secretary looked rather dubious, but made no objection.

"I'm on the first floor, Stacie, but we can take the lift."

The couple arrived at Basil's room within a minute.

"Come in, Stacie."

Stacie entered and looked round. The room was narrow; there was a single bed, beside which was a small set of drawers. At the end of the bed, against the wall, there was a wardrobe and by the window there was a small table, one armchair and one dining chair. Stacie noticed two photographs in frames on the window sill together with a brass box.

"It's not the Ritz, is it, Stacie?"

She didn't really know how to reply, so she merely smiled at Basil.

"Have a seat, dear. No, not that one – you take the armchair." Basil sat on the other chair. "What do you think, then?"

"Well, it's very compact, but the view from the window is nice."

"Definitely the room's best feature, wouldn't you say?"

"Is that your wife in the photos, Basil?"

"Yes – the one on the left was taken on our wedding day and the other a few months before she died."

"Is the brass box hers as well?"

"No, no, that belonged to my father – it contains his medals from

50

the First World War. My dad was fifty-five when I was born; my mum was his second wife, you see. I don't know what happened to his first. Would you like a look inside?"

Basil handed her the box. Before she opened it Stacie studied the lid.

"It's from Christmas 1914. And who's this young woman on the front?"

"Some member of the royal family, Stacie. She gave all the soldiers a Christmas present in the year the war started. My dad was in from the first day, you see. Open it up."

Stacie lifted the lid. Inside there were three medals and a strange metallic item.

"One of the medals is quite rare, Stacie – the one with the crown and the red, white and blue ribbon dates from 1914. My dad always called it the Mons Star. The other two were given to all soldiers at the end of the war."

"What was in the box, Basil?"

"I guess it was cigarettes because the metal thing is a lighter from the same period."

"Are they worth anything, Basil?"

"Yes, but I'm not sure exactly how much. I saw a similar set on one of those television auction shows; they sold for 100 smackers, but that was without the Mons Star. It's the only thing of any value that I brought with me here; I had to sell everything else to raise enough cash to pay for my keep. Hey, is that the time? We can go to the lounge for tea and cakes if you like."

"No, thanks, Basil. I'd better get back, but I'll see you here when I'm working, no doubt."

On her way back to the bungalow Stacie wondered if all the rooms were as sterile as Basil's.

Fifteen minutes later Stacie let herself into her temporary dwelling; she found Dave in the sitting room watching television.

"Hi, Dave, what are you watching?"

"It's one of them antiques programmes. Where have you been all this time?"

"Well, Dave, for some of the period I was examining a real antique."

Her lover turned to face her. "Where?"

51

"In the local care home – my friend Basil invited me to his room."

Dave frowned at her. "Oh yeah? For what?"

"Nothin' like that, darlin'; if you remember, you asked me to sus out the care home. I went there this morning to be briefed on the job, then later I met Basil and we went to the pub. The Matron had paid me cash in hand for two hours, so I was able to buy the old guy a drink; he invited me to visit his room, so I jumped at the opportunity."

"And?"

"Well, his room is very compact and the only things of value were some medals and a brass box from the First World War; he told me they were his father's. He reckoned they are worth 100 quid or so because he'd seen a TV programme, like the one you're watching now, when a set fetched that amount."

"OK, Stacie, that sounds promising."

"Yeah, and remember, Dave, that most of the other residents are women who probably have kept many more souvenirs than Basil – you know, jewellery and stuff."

Dave turned the sound down on the television.

"When do you start work there, Stacie?"

"The Matron will phone me – I've given her the landline number here and your mobile number. She reckons I'll be needed most days."

Dave thought for several seconds before explaining a possible development. "Look, try and get some night work there; you could let me in so I can take a butcher's. There may be larger items."

"There's one of them smart TVs in the lounge, Dave."

This was more like it! Dave turned up the sound again and gave his full attention to the programme.

CHAPTER 7

Samantha Fagan was up early the next day. For her first observation of activity at Chelford Town Recycling Centre she had decided to follow Tobias Argent's lead and appear early. She had her smartphone with its inbuilt camera to record comings and goings. Later she could make hard copy at her leisure; she could also perhaps be creative with the data to suit her and Tobias's ends.

She knew where the town tip was, but had never before visited in person – her father always dealt with excess garbage. Her first problem was to find a vantage point from where she could observe without staff at The Tip being aware of her presence or her task.

Chelford had a small industrial estate at the edge of town; The Tip was situated in the central area in a side street with one other business. Harley Dumpers hired out machines to the building trade, and its site overlooked The Tip's compound. Samantha arrived at eight thirty and walked up to the entrance of this other business, which was already in operation. She could see an office in which lights were shining; she noticed a window which would be a suitable observation post, but how could she gain access to it? As she considered the problem she noticed a very handsome young chap arrive at The Tip. The gate was locked, so he stood and waited. Samantha was in full view, so she had no alternative but to enter Harley Dumpers' yard?

"Can I help you, dear?" The question was posed by a middle-aged woman who had opened the office door.

Samantha had to think quickly – how would a politician answer in a potentially difficult situation? Of course, she thought, they would make something up that seemed to be for the common good.

"I wonder if you can help me, please? I'm here on behalf of the SOS organisation."

The woman was clearly nonplussed. "The what, dear?"

"The Staffordshire Ornithological Society. You see, we're recording observations of bird life across the county and we're particularly interested in industrial sites like this one, so I wonder if I could perhaps observe from your office? It looks like it might rain any minute and your office offers a high vantage point."

"Of course you can, dear. Our largest window is in our waiting room and we don't have any appointments this morning, so please come in. Actually, I do a spot of birdwatching myself; can you see that fine young cock waiting to enter The Tip?"

"Yes indeed – such a fine specimen! Is he a resident or a summer migrant, do you know?"

"I asked my friend Mollie who works down there; he's from Romania and he's done a lot for the recycling business, which is now visited by many young and not so young women, you won't be surprised to hear. Now I'll make us both a cup of tea and then I must start work. Just call me if you need anything."

Samantha turned to look out of the window. The cock had flown. The Tip's gate was open, but there wasn't a sign of anyone depositing rubbish.

Samantha stayed for one hour, in which time only two cars arrived. Each time the handsome Romanian appeared to offer his assistance. Samantha made sure she took photographs to record later on her data chart.

"How are you getting on, dear?"

Samantha turned to face the woman she had met earlier. "Oh, fine, thank you. I've seen several sparrows and a couple of crows."

"But have you seen the greater spotted rose finch? I see it quite often in the bush over to your left."

"I may have and I've definitely seen the handsome Romanian cock several times. However, there doesn't seem to be much business at The Tip today. Is it like this every Tuesday?"

"I don't look out often, dear, so really I can't say."

"Do you work here full-time, may I ask?"

"Yes, I've been the secretary here for fifteen years. I work from nine to five Monday to Friday and half-day on Saturdays."

"So you've seen things develop in the area?"

"Oh yes."

"Has the amount of recycling at The Tip increased, would you say?"

"Definitely. Sometimes on Saturday mornings there's a long queue of cars waiting to unload from opening time onwards."

Samantha suddenly remembered her made-up reason for being in the office.

"This waiting room is a marvellous place for birdwatching. Can I come again, please?"

"Yes, certainly. Just give me a ring so I can let the boss know. He's a bit fussy, so you'll have to sign in; he's not in today, fortunately. Now, can I have your name?"

"Oh, right, I'm Sally Fuller and I must be off now because I've got to visit a similar facility in Stafford."

As she walked away Samantha marvelled at her powers of improvisation, but she was not aware that Harley Dumpers' secretary was, at that very moment, attempting to phone her old friend Mollie Knowles at The Tip.

"Morning, Mollie. It's Nora here. I've had an interesting visitor this morning – someone called Sally Fuller, who claimed to be working for the SOS. She told me the initials stand for Staffordshire Ornithological Society. No, I've never heard of it either. Actually, Mollie, she seemed more interested in observing activity in your compound. She's definitely nothing to do with birdwatching – I know that because I set a little trap. I asked if she'd seen the greater spotted rose finch? Now, a genuine twitcher would have told me there is no such species; she didn't, so I bet she's working for someone else."

Mollie had listened to her friend Nora's information with growing interest.

"Is she coming again, Nora?"

"Yes, I've invited her back. And don't worry, I'll let you know when she's here. Who is she working for, do you think?"

55

"Either the council or our local MP. Keep this to yourself, Nora, but The Tip is in danger of either being sold off or closed down. I'll tell Jack Sugden what you've just told me so we can work something out. Thank you very much, Nora."

Mollie recognised that something serious was taking place, so she left the Portakabin and went to find Jack. As usual he was standing at the top of the ramp beside the residual-waste container.

"Jack, I need a word with you urgently."

"Can't it wait till my lunch break, Mollie?"

"Yes, if you insist, but I have some very important news linked to the recent monitoring visit."

"OK, Mollie, I'll just get Fred to take over from me here, then I'll come to the office."

Two minutes later he joined Mollie.

"What's up, Mollie?"

Slowly she reported what Nora had told her over the phone.

Jack took several seconds to respond to the news: "Some bugger is watching us, Mollie."

"Definitely, Jack, and I guess I know why."

Jack raised his eyebrows. "Well?"

"It'll be our illustrious MP, Jack. He wants to persuade the council to either privatise us or, worse, shut us down. This young woman, Sally Fuller – or whoever she is – has clearly been hired to find out how much business we do."

"How can we stop her, Mollie?"

"Well, one of us could sneak up behind her and stab her in the back."

"There's no need to be sarcastic, Mollie."

"Right. Well, my friend Nora will telephone me when this Sally turns up again at Harley Dumpers, so we will know we're being watched."

"What will you do, Mollie?"

"I don't know, that's why I'm telling you; clearly we need a plan."

"Shall we tell the lads?"

"Well, Jack, if we do it will hardly be a drip feed, will it? Now, you're the boss so it's your decision."

"What would you do, Mollie?"

"Oh no, Jack, not me – you're in charge. You decide. If I were you I'd think about it for the rest of this working day, but then, Jack, we need a plan."

"Right, Mollie."

Jack left the Portakabin looking confused.

"Let me know before we close, Jack," she called after him.

Mollie did not really expect a decision before the end of the working day and she was surprised when Jack came to see her just before closing time.

"I've asked the lads to call into the office for a few minutes when we knock off, Mollie."

"What are you going to drip-feed them, Jack?"

"Well, they need to know what's happening, so I thought I'd ask them for their ideas."

Mollie was about to protest, but the door opened and all the staff presented themselves.

"I won't keep you long, lads, but Mollie here has some important information for you."

'To drip-feed or not to drip-feed,' Mollie thought to herself while recognising she had been placed in the firing line.

She smiled at the assembled males and reported what Nora had told her.

"What do we do, Mollie?" Fred Urmston posed the question.

Mollie turned to Jack: "I believe you have the answer, Jack."

There was no time for Jack to duck because every eye was on him.

"Well, lads, I thought that, as you all could be affected, I'd listen to your ideas."

He didn't expect any, but to everyone's surprise Winston Green spoke up: "We need to provide false activity."

"That's really bright, that is." Fred Urmston had a definite gift for sarcasm.

"Let the lad speak, Fred."

Winston was surprised to receive Pete Fenton's support, so he continued: "This woman came early, so how about this: each day, when we knock off, we load some small electrical items into our car boots and take them home; next morning we park in the main road; then when Nora rings Mollie here we go to our cars and drive them here to The Tip and unload the items we loaded the night before as though we were genuine customers."

It took some time for Winston's idea to sink in.

Finally Fred rejected it: "No good, mate – the young cow would recognise us all."

"She wouldn't if we had balaclavas or big caps stored in our cars so that when we drove them here our faces would be covered."

Once again Winston's latest idea dripped into the assembled masculine grey matter.

"Someone would need to stay 'ere in case some real customers arrived." Dimitri had been quiet up to this point, but now he assaulted Fred's latest objection: "I'll remain here."

Winston was the victor.

"Right, lads, pick up some items now before you go in case the spy appears tomorrow."

'At last,' Mollie thought to herself, 'the boss has issued an order.'

As they loaded the cars Winston whispered to Fred, "Look, there's no one checking what we're loading, so when we unload we can keep a few items for sale later."

Fred had to admit to himself that the lad was sharp.

"When is your mate bringing his truck, Winston, so we can share 500 smackers?"

"Soon, Fred, but first we 'ave to get rid of the spy."

An opportunity to uncover the secret agent arrived two days later. Mollie was about to leave for work when she received a call from Nora.

"She's here, Mollie; she's had a good look into your compound and now she's walking slowly up towards my office. I'll invite her in, then I'll ring you again so you can come and meet her."

"Thanks, Nora. I'll inform the lads."

They say practice makes perfect, and the first part of the false activity went off well because the team had practised for two days. Staff had parked their cars in the main road. Dimitri opened the gates dead on time and went to his normal position; Jack, Fred, Pete and Mollie arrived by car about two minutes apart; Winston arrived later in Jack's wife's vehicle; Dimitri went to each in turn to offer help.

Most of the false customers remained in their cars. Fred Urmston was the exception – he had his anorak hood pulled up and he seemed to empty his car boot, but unbeknown to Jack and Mollie he left one microwave oven in situ. Once they had unloaded, the team drove back to the main road and then, one at a time, with heads covered, they returned to The Tip. On this day, however, Mollie walked past the main gate and trudged up the hill to meet Nora at Harley Dumpers.

Nora had continued to help the team pull off the scam, because she had invited Samantha into the waiting area again and offered her tea.

"I've got a potential customer arriving in a minute; you won't mind sharing this room with her, will you, Ms Fuller?"

"No, not at all," Samantha assured her. "Today I've brought my binoculars." As if to emphasise the fact, Samantha raised them to her eyes and directed them to the main window. "There seems to be plenty going on at The Tip today," Samantha announced, "but of course I'm here to observe the bird life. I hope to see that greater spotted finch thing today."

Nora made no comment because Mollie had now arrived.

"Good morning, Mrs Knowles. Nice to see you again. Can I introduce . . ."

Nora paused as though she had forgotten Samantha's false name.

The young woman attempted to help her out: "I'm Samantha. How do you—"

Nora interrupted her: "That's funny – the last time you were here I could swear you said your name was Sally."

Time for a political U-turn.

"Actually, I'm Samantha and Sally – my parents argued over my name when I was born. These days Mum calls me Samantha and Dad calls me Sally – it's all a bit confusing."

Mollie entered the conversation: "Are you here to hire a dumper, Samantha–Sally?"

"No, no, this kind lady lets me do some birdwatching for the SOS."

Mollie affected a quizzical expression.

Nora offered enlightenment: "SOS stands for Staffordshire Ornithological Society, Mrs Knowles."

"Really? I've never heard of it. Is the SOS on the Internet, Samantha?"

"Oh yes, Wikipedia, Facebook and Twitter."

Nora turned up the heat: "Now, that's very strange, Sally, because I've checked on all those sites; the SOS appears on none of them."

"Well, we're a very new organisation," Sally explained.

Mollie asked for further enlightenment: "Perhaps you are the only member, Sally?"

"Of course I'm not – and now I must leave."

Mollie and Nora formed themselves into a formidable barrier and blocked the exit.

Mollie became the spokesperson: "You are not a birdwatcher, young madam; you are here to spy on activity at The Tip. You see, there is no such bird as the greater spotted rose finch; any real birdwatcher would know that. You are working for someone other than the fictional SOS, and I believe I know who. Now you need to tell him you've been rumbled. And yes, please leave and don't come back. Incidentally, that is a warning not mere advice."

Mollie and her friend each turned sideways so a very frustrated Tory could leave.

When Mollie and Nora were alone Nora expressed her opinion of what would happen in the near future: "She, or someone else, will be back, Mollie – politicians are always on the lookout to further their own careers."

"You're right, of course, Nora, but, oh boy, I did enjoy that!"

Samantha–Sally knew she had a problem, but she was determined not to let Tobias know she had been rumbled. She had some data, and now was the time, surely, to be creative with it – in the best political tradition, of course.

CHAPTER 8

Stacie was hot and bothered. She had received an early morning call from Matron and now she was standing in the care home's cramped laundry room, where the heat and steam were almost overpowering. She wasn't alone. Joan Setters, a permanent member of staff, was about to explain her duties.

"Have you worked in a laundry before, dear?"

Stacie shook her head.

"Well, it's dead easy really. When this washer has finished you take out the sheets using this basket and you take them to the tumble dryer next to the window. You stick them in and turn the dial to the 'easy iron' setting and you put the exhaust pipe out of the window. Next you reload the washer with more sheets using the 'cotton' setting and then you wait."

"Is that all I do, Mrs Setters?"

"No, dear, you also do the pressing."

Stacie hadn't a clue what this meant.

"Sorry, Mrs Setters – I don't understand."

"That's all right, dear, I didn't when I started 'ere. Next door, see, is the pressing room. Look, come with me now and I'll show you."

Stacie followed the expert. Out in the corridor the air was much fresher, but Stacie could feel sweat dripping from her armpits.

The pressing room was equally cramped, but at least it was cooler. Stacie puffed out her cheeks and breathed out noisily.

"It's cooler in 'ere, dear, but the laundry room is good for you." Stacie must have looked astonished because Joan Setters immediately clarified her comment: "No one who works in the laundry ever gets sinus trouble – rheumatism, yes."

The pressing room was dominated by a huge electric press.

"Now, dear, you put the bed sheets on the machine's flat surface; you lower the press lid and switch it on. Watch for this red light carefully. Once it comes on lift the press and remove the sheet; fold it carefully so it doesn't crease – Matron won't have creases. Now, 'ave you got all that?"

"Yes, thanks."

"Right – good. Now I've got to go and help the cook, so I'll leave you to it."

Stacie's day passed by in heat, vapour and boredom and she began to wonder if she would ever have to return to this oppressive torture in the future. She felt isolated and her head ached with the incessant noises of the three machines. Her only relief was when she had to leave the laundry for the pressing room, but she saw no one in the corridor. Her mind wandered so much that she once forgot to watch for the red light and she was jerked from her reverie by a loud warning signal from the machine. Even then no one came to check.

The steam in the laundry developed to a fog-like density by mid afternoon and Stacie's consciousness became dreamlike. Suddenly, without warning, a pair of legs appeared before her and, as the steam cleared a little, a face came into view.

Stacie gasped and the face spoke: "I have been sent to help you."

Stacie's whole body was shaking. Was she in a horror film?

"Who are you?" she asked in a faltering voice.

What or whoever it was stepped forward towards her; she stepped back until she was pressed against the laundry wall. Out of the mist stepped one of the most handsome men she had ever met.

"I am Dimitri. I am from Romania."

'Oh, my God!' Stacie thought. 'That's where Dracula came from.'

"I'm sorry to have startled you, miss, but Matron has sent me."

Stacie's heartbeat slowed a little.

"Oh, right – could you take some ironed sheets up to the bedroom, please?"

"Are you all right, miss?"

"Yes, I'm OK – you startled me a bit, that's all."

"I am so sorry. Where are the sheets?"

"Next door in the pressing room. Please follow me."

By now Stacie had a full view of Dracula. He was a superb specimen: six feet two, eyes so brown, voice so deep, body so slim and muscular.

"Have you worked here long, miss?"

"No, this is my first day. I'm Stacie, by the way."

"It is my first day also, but I can only work here on Wednesday and Thursday; I have another job, you see."

"Really? Where?"

"At the Chelford recycling facility."

"Do you like it there?"

"Oh yes, I am learning about waste all the time, and when I return home I hope to start my own recycling business. I think you have been given a very difficult job here. It would be far better if I work down here whilst you work in the old people's rooms."

Stacie totally agreed with him.

"Thank you, but who do we ask?"

"I will approach the member of staff called Sami – he seems a very reasonable person. I will go now."

Stacie watched him leave before leaning back against the wall again, but this time in ecstasy, not fear. It suddenly struck her that working in the bedrooms would give her opportunities to see which residents had the most valuable items.

Joan Setters came to the laundry close to the end of Stacie's shift.

"Right, dear, I've brought your pay. Can you come again tomorrow because we're still short of staff?"

"Er, yes."

"Good. Now, tomorrow Matron wants you to help me cleaning the bedrooms and the lounge; that smashing bloke you've met will work down here."

"That's great – thank you."

Stacie walked home with her head held high. There had been very few occasions in her life when her endeavours had been appreciated. Her mood changed when Dave confronted her at the bungalow.

"Where the 'ell have you been all this time?"

Stacie opened her purse and pulled out her day's earnings.

"Well, that's not much for a day's work."

Stacie agreed with her partner's assessment, but she looked on the bright side.

"They've paid me the minimum wage, Dave, and I'm working again tomorrow." These facts mellowed Dave's attitude, so Stacie asked him about his day: "What have you been up to, then, Dave?"

"I've spent hours trying to contact Denny. I sent him texts and I've even rung his mobile."

Stacie did not dare show her satisfaction; instead she asked another question: "What do you think has happened to him?"

"I don't bloody know and I'm not ringing him again in case someone has nicked his phone. What's for tea?"

"I thought we could eat at that pub because I'll be paid again tomorrow."

"What do you have to do, Stacie?"

"Today I had to work in the laundry, but tomorrow I'm going to help clean the residents' rooms – you know what that means, don't you, Dave?"

"Yeah, you'll be able to find out where the goodies are." Stacie could see that Dave was definitely upbeat. "Come on, Stacie, we're going to that pub."

This decision proved his mood had changed.

Samantha, sometimes Sally, was considering her next move. She had to present a convincing set of data to Tobias that would suit his political ambition. Her birdwatching scam had fallen from its nest, and so far she had very few actual recorded facts. It was time to involve the family.

She called out to her father, "Dad, there's a load of unwanted stuff in the garage. Can I help you dispose of it at The Tip?"

"Oh, thanks, Sammy. I've got some free time at the

moment. I'm not sure when The Tip opens, but we can certainly load the car."

"Yeah, let's do that, Dad. Then I'll drive it round to the facility to find out the opening times. If they're shut today the stuff can stay in the boot, can't it?"

"Yes – no problem, Sammy."

Actually, Samantha was well aware that The Tip was closed, but she welcomed an opportunity to examine the immediate surrounding area with a view to finding a second, more suitable, observation point.

She arrived at The Tip within twenty minutes and parked her car immediately before the locked gates; she got out and gazed into the compound. At first it seemed that her visit would be wasted time, but on her last sweeping gaze something significant caught her eye. Above the Portakabin door she noticed a CCTV camera. She had no doubt that the device would hold a treasure trove of relevant data, but there was one problem: how could she gain access? She drove off with the problem unresolved.

Samantha's visit had not gone unnoticed: Nora Stubbins spotted her presence when greeting a potential customer.

At the end of the working day Nora phoned Mollie.

"Is that you, Mollie? Nora here."

"What's up, Nora?"

"The false birdwatcher has been to The Tip again."

"Oh dear – pity it's shut."

"She spent some time looking into the compound, Mollie."

"She must have a rubbish obsession! Did she have any recyclable stuff with her, do you know?"

"I couldn't see anything from my window, but she stayed parked at the main gate for some time."

"What do you think she's up to, Nora?"

"Well, she wasn't birdwatching, that's for sure."

"Perhaps she hoped to encounter the greater Romanian cock, Nora."

"Maybe. But hang on a minute, does The Tip have CCTV?"

"Yes, but no one ever checks the tape. We've never had a break-in during my time, you see."

"But there will be a visual record, won't there? I bet she tries to get her claws on it."

Mollie could see that her friend had a valid point.

"I'll contact Jack straight away, Nora. And thanks very much for your help."

Mollie rang Jack's home number, but there was no reply. She wondered about leaving a message, but decided against – tomorrow would be soon enough to tell him the worrying news.

In the event Jack phoned her next morning at ten o'clock.

"Mollie, I've had a call from George Rampling."

"But it's your day off, Jack."

"I know that, but he's insisted he meets me at The Tip at noon today."

"Why, Jack?"

"All he said was that he needs to meet me urgently."

"Right, but why are you ringing me?"

"Could you be there when he comes, Mollie? It's always better when there are two of us. I'm pretty sure it will be about cutting costs."

Mollie remembered Nora's insight about the CCTV camera.

"Righto, Jack; I'll come right now because there's something important I need to share with you."

"Thanks, Mollie. See you soon."

Nora Stubbins was surprised when she heard two cars arrive at The Tip on a day when it was shut. She looked out of her window and recognised both vehicles. She watched as Jack opened up, but any further observations were blocked by her boss, who called her into his office.

"What is it you need to share with me, Mollie?" Jack asked this as he and Mollie prepared themselves cups of tea.

"Nora, who works up at Harley Dumpers, she's a friend of mine, you know . . ."

Jack did know and showed his impatience with one word: "Well?"

"She saw the birdwatcher studying The Tip from the main gate yesterday."

"Mollie, the place was shut yesterday, and anyway she might

have genuinely brought some items for recycling and got the wrong date."

"And, Jack, she may have been trying to spot a weak point."

"Possibly, but I doubt it."

"Nora asked me if we have CCTV, Jack."

"Well, of course – Oh, my God, we forgot about it!"

"It still works, Jack, and there'll be recent footage. Just imagine the damage to us if it gets into the wrong hands."

"What the hell do we do, Mollie?"

"I've got an idea, Jack. As we never check it and we've never been broken into why don't we say to Mr Rampling that we can save money by dismantling it? My guess is that lowering costs will be the focus of his visit. He's due very shortly, isn't he?"

"Good idea, Mollie. Do you know how to erase the recording?"

"I have the manual in my desk, Jack. I'll get it out now."

George Rampling arrived at noon on the dot. He was surprised when Mollie opened the Portakabin door to welcome him.

"Is Jack Sugden here, please? I phoned him earlier."

"Yes, Mr Rampling. He's just washing his hands – come in and have a seat."

"Who invited you, Mrs Knowles? It certainly wasn't me."

Mollie had no chance to answer Rampling because her colleague appeared briskly rubbing his hands on a paper towel.

"Ah, there you are, Jack. I was just asking Mrs Knowles here why she is here as well."

Jack was stuck for an answer.

Mollie took the initiative: "If you remember, Jack, you phoned me earlier and asked me to be present so that I could take notes at what could be a very important meeting."

Jack relaxed a little.

"That's right, Mr Rampling – I hope you don't mind."

"No, it's quite a good idea actually because a typed-up record might come in very useful when I meet local councillors. Mrs Knowles's notes will prove that we have given serious consideration to future developments at this recycling facility."

Jack smelled a rat.

"Which future developments are those, Mr Rampling?"

"My department is under tremendous pressure to save money, Jack. All council services and facilities have been set savings targets, and if I can't come up with a plan I will have cuts imposed. Now I'm here to ask you for any ideas you might have."

George Rampling did not expect any response at this stage; in fact, his reasons for the visit were to drip-feed some bad news while seeking to involve those employed in permanent posts.

He was therefore very surprised when Mollie Knowles spoke up: "We know there's a problem, Mr Rampling, and we have one idea as to how we can cut a cost here."

"Really, Mrs Knowles? How?"

Mollie didn't respond; instead she turned to the supervisor: "You explain, please, Jack."

"Oh, right, well, see, Mr Rampling, we have CCTV which we never use; it's switched on, of course, but we've never had a break-in so really the system is redundant."

Mollie was eager to be more specific: "There have to be several savings, Mr Rampling – electricity and maintenance, to name but two."

"Well, thank you both for that idea. I shall certainly include it in my provisional plan; however, any savings are likely to be small. What councillors are really looking for are job cuts. Now, I know you have recently acquired two new recruits so my question is this: do you really need them? I ask this with a view to maintaining all experienced staff, like yourselves. George Rampling could almost feel the relief surging through Jack and Mollie.

"Would they both have to go, Mr Rampling?"

"No, not both of them immediately, Mrs Knowles; one would suffice for a few months, say. Now, you know the men involved so you are well placed to judge their individual worth; therefore I believe you, Jack, as supervisor, should make the decision, which I need to know by this time next week. Now, any more queries before I go?"

It was clear from his attitude that the last thing George Rampling wanted, at this juncture, was any more questions.

He waited two seconds before he made his exit.

"He's dumped a problem on you, Jack."

"I'm quite aware of that, thank you, Mollie."

"So who out of Winston and Dimitri will you choose for the push?"

Jack did not answer because he was, for once, deep in thought.

"Who would you pick Mollie?"

The administrator recognised a potential trap.

"Perhaps it would be better to take a joint decision made by all the experienced staff."

Jack felt a surge of relief.

"Good idea, Mollie! Now, I'll tell you what, let's contact Fred and Pete today and ask them to arrive half an hour early for work tomorrow. Say it's very important."

"So you want me to make the calls, then, Jack?"

"Well, you are the administrator."

"OK, I'll hand you the CCTV manual so that, as supervisor, you can erase all the footage."

Jack was unsure, but then he remembered that George Rampling had been informed and had seemed to agree with the potential cost savings.

CHAPTER 9

Samantha Fagan, also known as Sally Fuller, was preparing for her meeting with Tobias Argent. Her data collection had not gone well, but she had at least made one visit to the Chelford tip in the company of her father. He had emptied the car boot while she took the opportunity to observe, first-hand, the systems in use. She had her smartphone and was therefore able to take photographs. There was only one other vehicle in the compound and she noticed the Romanian cock helping an elderly gent unload large bags of garden rubbish; all other staff members were standing around doing nothing. Samantha took several shots, including one of a staff member who appeared to be lifting something from the container marked as being for small electrical items. Samantha walked towards the container to obtain a clearer view; as she did so she passed a large metallic shed-like container which housed large electrical items. She looked inside and saw unwanted washing machines, tumble dryers and fridges. She also noticed that three washing machines had been placed behind the container.

"Can I help you, miss?"

Samantha turned and came face to chest with the cock.

"Oh, er, no, thank you. It's my first visit and I'm just looking around – finding my bearings, so to speak."

"If you need more information, Mr Sugden is the expert. You'll find him by the residual-waste container, miss."

"Oh, right, thank you. But actually I think my father is ready to leave now."

"Goodbye, miss. I hope to see you again."

'And I you,' Samantha thought to herself.

Later, at home, Samantha became creative with her meagre amount of data. She trebled her observations from Harley Dumpers imaginatively, then she printed off photographs taken when she had visited The Tip on her own and she made several copies of those taken when she had visited The Tip with her father.

Tobias had chosen the Chelford Conservative Club for his second meeting with Samantha. He had no doubt that she would have obtained damning evidence of business – or preferably lack of it – at The Tip, and he really wasn't bothered if news got out; indeed such a leak might help because some staff might resign. With these considerations in mind, he waited for Samantha in the main public area.

"Ah, there you are, young lady. Now, what have you got for me?"

"Good afternoon, Tobias."

The MP cut her short: "Here you must address me as Mr Argent."

"I'm so sorry, Mr Argent. Now, I have a numerical breakdown on this Microsoft Excel document and I have photographs – some taken from a vantage point, others from within the compound itself. If you like I can explain the numerical data first. "

"Very good, Miss Fagan, but I'll start with the pictures."

Samantha passed them to him while remembering a line from Shakespeare's *Coriolanus*, which she had studied in school. The bard had written, 'The eyes of the ignorant are more learned that the ears.' Mr Argent's eyes certainly had it.

"Excellent, Miss Fagan! This is exactly the evidence I need. I shall take these to my next meeting with relevant councillors."

"I did think about emailing it all to you, Mr Argent."

"I'm so glad you didn't, because I can use all of it as a shock tactic. Now listen – my main political agent is approaching retirement, so soon I will need a replacement. Would you be interested?"

"I certainly would, sir."

Next morning both Fred Urmston and Pete Fenton arrived early for work; neither was in a happy mood.

"This really had better be important, Jack, because Pete and I insist on being paid for all the time we spend here."

Jack remained grim-faced for once.

"I was called to a meeting yesterday, lads, on my day off, and I won't get any pay for it."

"Who the 'ell made you come 'ere on your day off, Jack?"

Jack turned to face Pete Fenton; the time for drip-feeding was over.

"George Rampling, and he told me that we've got to lose staff; Mollie will back up what I'm saying."

"I was present as well, lads, so what Jack is about to tell you is absolutely true."

"Someone has to be fired because the local authority has been set a savings target," Jack explained. "Now, Mollie and I came up with one suggestion to save money, but Rampling said it was not enough."

"What was your suggestion, then?"

"Well, Fred, we suggested that we do not need CCTV coverage."

Both Jack and Mollie were surprised by the confused expressions on their colleagues' faces.

"We 'aven't got CCTV, 'ave we? I've never noticed a camera."

Mollie explained the situation: "It's been here, Fred, from the day TheTip opened. The camera is situated on this Portakabin, but don't worry – Jack and I have erased all the footage."

Mollie and Jack were surprised again, but this time by the looks of utter relief which swept across two weathered faces.

"Who's got to go, then, Jack?"

"Fred, you'll be relieved to know that it won't be one of us here now. We are experienced staff, but, of course, we have two new men."

"Are you making the decision, then, Jack?"

"Well, Pete, you know me – I like to lead as happy a team as possible, so I would like your opinions on who should go."

Jack wasn't surprised when both Fred and Pete named Dimitri; Mollie wasn't happy, however.

"Why are you two picking on Dimi? He's a much more reliable worker than Winston, who, I remind you, is often late."

The assembled males knew this was true, so Fred tried the patriotic tack: "Yeah, but at least he's British – I mean, Dimi is one of them emigrants that's come over 'ere to take one of our jobs."

"I would remind you, Fred Urmston, that several of our countrymen have let us down recently, and I remind you also that business has picked up because of Dimitri's professionalism."

Fred was having none of Mollie's argument: "OK, we've had a few more women coming because they want to see the foreign hunk, but surely we can't kick out a Brit even if he does come from London."

Mollie had had enough: "Right, Jack, over to you. You've heard the debate, now we need a decision."

Jack pondered: why was it he was always being placed on the spot? Democracy was called for.

"Right, thank you, everyone. Now I suggest we put it to a vote. I shall act as the speaker, so I won't take part; now, those of you in favour of keeping Winston please raise your hands."

Fred and Pete registered their votes.

"Those in favour of Dimi."

"Jack, we can leave it there. I'm the only remaining voter, aren't I?"

Of course Mollie was right – the decision was made: the Romanian had to go.

"Who's going to tell him, Jack?"

"Well, Fred, I suggest Mollie and I wait till knocking-off time, then we can invite him to the office."

"Oh no, Jack. You are the supervisor – you tell him."

Jack was about to object, but was interrupted by someone knocking at the door. It was Dimitri, who had arrived for work; there was no sign yet of Winston. Dimitri was confused because he was usually the first to arrive; today everyone, apart from Winston, of course, had turned up before him. Mollie spotted his anxiety.

"We've had an important staff meeting, Dimi; Jack will tell

you and Winston the details later today."

Dimitri turned to face Jack, who, as usual, took the easy way out: "Mollie's right, Dimi. I can't tell you anything now because we all have to go to our positions. Has Winston arrived yet?"

No one replied.

Winston finally arrived when The Tip had been open for ten minutes. He made sure he was running as he came through the main gate. Fortunately for him Jack was in the toilet; so he rushed to his usual position, where he was approached by both Fred and Pete.

"You're late again, mate, aren't you?"

"Sorry about that, Fred, but my alarm didn't go off."

"You've used that excuse before, Winston." This time it was Pete who wasn't satisfied. "We two have done you a bloody great favour, mate."

"Really, Fred? What was it?"

"Pete, you go to your normal position while I explain to matey boy 'ere."

Fred took Winston's arm and led him behind the large-electrical-items container.

When they were out of sight Fred began his explanation: "Jack told us earlier today that someone has to lose their job 'ere. It came down to you or Dimi because you two are not experienced staff, see. Well, we had a vote and you won."

"Do you mean I can stay?"

"Exactly that, matey, and I guess you know why."

"You mean about the 500 quid, Fred?"

"Too right, matey! Now, when is your friend from London coming to collect the stuff? It's all ready for him, as you know. You see, Winston, really Pete and I should have voted for the Romanian – he's a damn sight more reliable than you."

"OK, OK, I'll contact my mate Joey Miller later today. Have you got a key to open up when he arrives?"

"No problem, Winston, but don't fail us or else me and Pete might have to say we think you're a crook to Jack. He'll believe us, matey."

"OK."

Fred looked out carefully from their hiding place. Dimitri and Pete were helping customers empty three vehicles; Jack was up by the residual-waste container talking to someone else.

"Quick, matey – let's go."

Fred assumed their chat had gone unnoticed, but he was wrong. Mollie had seen them both hide and leave. She made a note of her observation, including the date and time.

"Please, Mollie, be here when I tell Dimitri he's being sacked."

It was close to the end of the working day and Jack was feeling distinctly uncomfortable.

"All right, Jack, I'll sit by my desk, but I'm not going to say anything."

Dimitri entered two minutes later.

"You wanted to see me, sir."

"Yes, that's right. Now, I'm sorry, but I have some bad news. We have to lose a member of staff, you see."

"And it's me?"

"Yes, Dimitri. I'm sorry, but it is you. We have to make savings, you see."

"May I ask why me? I have the same status as Winston, I believe."

"That is true, Dimitri."

"Well, sir, have you asked Winston if we could each work half-time, thus saving one whole job?"

Jack was caught with his intellect down.

"Er, no." He turned to Mollie: "We didn't, did we, Mollie?"

Mollie broke her silence, despite her earlier resolution: "No, Jack, we didn't. If you remember, you used a democratic method whereby all experienced staff had a vote."

Jack felt a sense of relief.

"Yes, Dimitri, that's what we did, so you see the process was absolutely fair."

To Jack and Mollie's surprise the handsome foreigner merely smiled at them. "I understand completely. When do I have to leave?"

Mollie intervened: "You can stay till the end of the month, Dimi. That should give you time to find another job perhaps."

"Perhaps, Mrs Knowles. Thank you for telling me, and now I must go."

Mollie noticed the drooped shoulders as Dimitri made his exit.

"Mollie, we don't know the council will pay him till the end of the month."

"Well they damn well ought to, Jack."

Dimitri began to walk back to the hostel alone deep in thought. Should he go back to London? Should he return to Romania? He dismissed both these possibilities.

His thought process was brought to an end by a vaguely familiar voice: "Hi there. You look fed up – can I help at all?"

He turned to his right and came face to smoke with the small young woman he had already met at the care home. She was smoking a cigarette outside The Red Lion pub.

"Oh, good evening. I'm not too well actually – my job is about to end."

"You've been given the push? Surely not!"

"Yes, it's true – I've got till the end of the month."

"What are you going to do?"

"I don't know at this minute."

"Why don't you try to get some more work at the local care home?"

"You are Stacie, I believe. Well, Stacie, I really need something permanent because I send money home to my parents every month."

"Well, look, when I've finished this fag, why don't you come with me to the care home? I'm due there at six o'clock. You could speak to Sami."

Dimitri recognised that this suggestion was worth a try.

"Yes, OK, I'll come with you."

Stacie stubbed out her cigarette on the ground.

"I've just got to say goodbye to my friend in the bar, Dimitri, then I'll be with you; you carry on."

She made sure Dimitri was on his way before she went back inside The Red Lion because she did not want Dave to see her with another male – especially one much more handsome than him. Dave was a very jealous type. He had finished his cigarette some minutes earlier and had gone to the Gents.

Stacie caught up with Dimitri at the entrance to the Town End Care Home, so they entered together. Sami was on duty in the reception area. He was expecting Stacie, but Dimitri's presence caused some confusion.

"We haven't hired you this evening, have we, Dimitri?"

"No, I'm here to see if I can be employed on a permanent basis."

Sami looked doubtful.

"I don't think that will be possible; but I tell you what, I'll go now and ask Matron – she's still on the premises."

"Oh, thank you." Stacie smiled at her new friend. "Good luck, Dimitri – I've got to go now and start work."

June Bailey, the Matron, was poring over the latest financial statement when Sami entered her office. She hated this aspect of her job. She had been trained to care for the elderly and the infirm, not to analyse financial data, so she was quite relieved when Sami appeared before her.

"Any problems, Sami? Has that young cleaner arrived?"

Her second in command reassured her: "Everything is running smoothly this evening, Matron."

She adopted a quizzical manner. "So?"

"I've got a young chap in reception – he's looking for a permanent job. He's worked here before and made a good impression."

"It's not a question of impressions, Sami; it all comes down to finance, and we're almost broke."

"May I remind you, Matron, that Imran is about to go on leave."

"Oh, hell, yes! I'd forgotten that – how long is he away?"

"A fortnight – without pay, of course."

Matron's brain clicked into calculation mode: "So if we hire this fellow, Sami, we can pay him less than Imran?"

"Without doubt, Matron."

"Right, show him in."

Sami returned to reception with a smile on his face.

"Matron will speak to you now, Dimitri – I think she has some good news for you."

Matron was sitting at her desk when Dimitri entered her office.

"Sit down, young man. Now, Sami tells me you are looking for full-time work in the near future."

"Yes, Matron, and a permanent contract if possible."

"You have worked here before, I believe."

"Yes, Matron, in the laundry and as a cleaner."

"So you have some idea of how we operate and the challenges we face?"

"Yes, just a little."

Matron was beginning to warm to East European charm.

"I can offer you permanent work for two weeks starting at the end of the month; I may be able to extend it, but I can't promise. Now, are you still interested?"

Dimitri thought quickly: two weeks' pay was better than hunger.

"Yes, Matron, I will take it."

"You will need some training, of course."

"I can be here on Tuesdays and Wednesdays all day, Matron."

"Excellent, but I can't pay you on training days."

"No problem, Matron. Thank you very much for the offer."

CHAPTER 10

The business transaction was all arranged. Winston had conferred with his workmates to arrange a date and time when all three of them could be available, and he had then spoken to Joey Miller, known as the Count, his contact in London. Joey had demanded a full description of the white goods on offer. At first he wasn't satisfied, but he changed his mind when Winston included a large fridge-freezer which was less than three years old.

"Right, mate, I'll see you tomorrow night about midnight."

"Do you need any instructions to find the place, Joey?"

"No, mate, I'll use old Dotty Satnav. See you soon."

Next day the working atmosphere at The Tip was depressed because all the men felt some guilt about Dimitri's dismissal. His male colleagues kept away from him as much as possible, and only Mollie was keen to speak to him. She, of course, had no sense of guilt; her main emotion was sympathy. To everyone's surprise, however, Dimitri seemed completely unaffected by his fate. He turned up for work early as usual, and he seemed to bear no grudge against any of his co-workers. Mollie spoke to him on the day the robbery was due to happen.

"How are you, Dimitri? Any luck finding a new job?"

"Yes, Mrs Knowles. I have been offered a fortnight's work full-time at the local care home."

"Anything after that?"

"No, nothing definite, although the Matron has told me

there might be an opening in the future."

Mollie guessed that the Matron, like her, was eager to support a pleasant, good-looking young man.

She entered the support arena: "Look, Dimi, I may be able to help you: I'll ring my friend at Harley Dumpers. That firm may have a vacancy."

"Oh, thank you, Mrs Knowles. I'm keen to stay in the recycling business so I can learn, and hopefully later I can start my own business in Romania."

Mollie was eager to find out more, but the phone cut her short.

"I must take this, Dimitri."

"And I must start work Mrs Knowles."

George Rampling's secretary was on the line: "Is that the Chelford recycling centre?"

"Yes, it is. Can I help you?"

"I'm ringing on behalf of George Rampling in Environment. He's asked me to tell you that an electrical engineer will visit the centre tomorrow and remove your CCTV installation. Will that be convenient for you?"

Mollie assured her that it would be before putting the phone down and making a note that she must inform Jack during his lunch break.

It was a warm springlike day and Mollie found Jack sitting with Fred Urmston in the sunshine.

"Sorry to interrupt your sunbathing, chaps, but I must pass on a message from George Rampling."

This name had a galvanising effect. Both men looked hard at Mollie.

"Did he say what it's about, Mollie?"

"Well, I spoke to his secretary, Jack. She told me that Herr Rampling has organised the complete removal of our CCTV system."

To her surprise Fred showed more interest than Jack: "Did she say when, Mollie?"

"Sometime tomorrow, Fred."

"Not today, then?"

"No, Fred. Like I told you, sometime tomorrow."

"Is something bothering you, Fred?"

"No, not really, Jack; it's just good to know when things happen."

Mollie was as surprised as Jack by Fred's last remark because neither of them had noticed Fred showing much interest in happenings at The Tip over the years. Mollie went back to the office, leaving the males to their sandwiches.

"Well, Fred, old Rampling has accepted my suggestion to remove our CCTV. I mean, if you think about it there are several savings."

"How do you mean, Jack?"

"Well, there are savings on both electric and maintenance, not to mention the fact that the system is still in working order, so it can be recycled."

"It's switched off now, isn't it, Jack?"

"Yeah, I cleared it the other day."

"So there'll be nothing on the tape, then."

"No, mate, it's dead to the world. Oh 'eck, is that the time? Come on, Fred, it's time we took over from the others so they can 'ave lunch."

The rest of the day passed without incident or questions. Business was very slack, so Mollie had time to ring her friend Nora at Harley Dumpers.

"Have you got any jobs available at the moment, Nora?"

"No, love. Now, don't tell me you're fed up working with all those handsome brutes."

"There's only one handsome brute, Nora, and he's been given the push."

"Surely not the Romanian hunk?"

"I'm afraid so. We've got to cut costs, so he's the chosen sacrifice. That's why I'm trying to help him. He's keen, he's bright and he's lovely."

"Well, I'll ask my boss, Mollie, but I doubt whether we can offer him anything. There are a lot round here that would say he's taking one of our jobs."

"Nora, I wish the other males here would go to Romania and take four of their jobs."

"No hope of that, eh, Mollie? None of them speak decent English never mind learning another language. I'll let you know tomorrow what my boss says."

At the end of the working day Mollie noticed that three of her co-workers were having an intense discussion. Winston was obviously taking the lead while Fred and Pete listened to him intently. Dimitri had left the premises and Jack was probably in the toilet. In Mollie's experience the circumstance was unique because normally Winston, Fred and Pete were off like the shots of three separate guns at five o'clock on the dot. Mollie would have been shocked if she could have heard what the men were discussing.

"Right, lads, my mate Joey will be here tonight at about midnight; he'll meet us in Brookhouse Road."

"Why not 'ere, Winston?"

"He's very cagey, Pete, because he's been inside twice. When he meets us we'll all get in his truck and he'll drive us here; he wants us to wear face masks."

"'Ave you told 'im there's no CCTV?"

"Yes, Fred, I have, but he's insistent; he's even going to cover the truck's registration plates before driving us all here. Fred, you can open up, then Joey will back in. I'll direct him to where the stuff is – we'll help him load up and then he'll leave. He should be away in about twenty minutes."

Fred was not happy. "Hang on a bit, Winston – when do we get the 500 quid?"

"He'll have it with him, Fred; when the gear's loaded he'll slip me an envelope."

"And we will count the cash before he leaves." Fred was adamant.

Winston had an idea: "Right, if we all get back in the truck, Joey can drive us to Brookhouse Road, and while he uncovers the registration plates we can count the cash and share it out. How's that?"

"Sounds OK to me, Winston. What about you, Pete?"

Pete had had some difficulty following Winston's suggestion and he had another problem: "I've got a calculator at 'ome and last night I used it to divide 500 quid by three. The answer came to one 'undred and sixty-six pounds and loads of pence. How are we goin' to sort that out in Brookhouse Road?"

Both Winston and Fred were struck dumb for a few seconds before Winston made another suggestion: "Right, we'll stay together and find a safe place to share the cash out."

"OK, but where?" Fred asked the pertinent question. "How about we come back to The Tip and sort it out in the office?"

"I haven't got a key to the office, Fred," said Winston.

Pete then tried to be useful: "Why don't we go to the snug bar at The Red Cat?"

Fred was exasperated: "The bloody Red Cat will be shut, Pete; just remember, it'll be after midnight."

"I know – we can use the toilets in the main town car park; no one will be using them that late, surely."

"Don't bank on that, Fred – I've 'ad a pee in them at one in the morning."

Fred tried another tack: "Now look, can you two trust me to look after the cash till tomorrow? We can nip to the snug at lunchtime and share it out."

Neither Winston nor Pete was happy with this proposal.

Pete voiced their joint concern: "Sorry, mate – that's not on."

Winston recognised the heart of the problem – they did not trust each other – but he believed he had the solution to end their mutual worries: "How about this: when Joey has driven off we come back here to The Tip and we put the cash overnight in a small electrical item, like a microwave, which we hide so we can all know where it is? We have the key to The Tip and we know there is no CCTV. We can all be present when we recover the loot tomorrow."

The other two gave the suggestion careful thought.

"What do you think, Pete?"

"Well, OK, we can wait till Jack and Mollie are at lunch and then find the stash and share it out."

All three recognised that the plan was not perfect, but it was the best they could come up with in the circumstances."

It was now well past the end of the working day; Jack and Mollie were the last to leave.

"Well, Jack, we've had a quiet day."

"We sure have, Mollie, and let's hope the situation will continue."

The situation did continue for the rest of the evening and even into the next day. The Count turned up just before midnight and his plan for deception and robbery seemed to work perfectly: the team loaded the agreed items on to his truck within twenty minutes. Joey almost drove off without paying his co-conspirators; Fred, however, grabbed him as he was climbing into the driver's cab.

"Eh, mate, aren't you forgetting something?"

"I'm just getting into the cab so I can get the cash from the glove compartment."

Pete and Winston stood in front of the truck as Joey handed an envelope to Fred.

"It's all there."

Fred opened the envelope and flicked through the notes; despite the poor light he reckoned that everything was in order.

Winston called up to Joey, "We can do this again, Joey."

Joey smiled down at him. "OK, Winston, send me a text when you're ready."

He started the engine and the others stood aside as he raced off into the night.

Fred now took the lead: "Right, lads, let's go and hide the cash in the agreed place. It was dead simple, wasn't it, and Winston could have put us on to a nice little earner?"

Pete soon found a small microwave oven in the small-electrical items container, then he and Winston watched carefully as Fred inserted the cash, still in its envelope.

"Where can we hide the microwave, lads?"

Pete had the answer: "Put it under the ramp near the ground, Fred – it'll be easy to fish out tomorrow."

Winston and Fred agreed and so the threesome left The Tip with smiles on their faces.

The following day started calmly enough. Fred, Pete and Winston were not worried when they saw that the small-electrical-items container was being emptied by a dumper truck; this wasn't a problem because the microwave was safely stashed under the ramp and they could claim later, if necessary, that it had been left there by mistake. They would only say this after they had removed the cash, of course.

Mollie was sitting at her desk filing her nails when she saw a van enter the compound; it stopped by her office door and a workman got out.

Mollie opened her window and called out to him, "Can I help you?"

"Is this the Chelford recycling centre, duck?"

'Poor chap!' Mollie thought to herself. 'Perhaps he can't read the large notice at the entrance.'

But she replied politely enough, "Yes, it is; you've found it – well done."

"I've come to remove your CCTV system; can I come in?"

"Yes, please do."

She watched as a short, plump, balding electrical engineer approached her.

"Could you make us a cup of tea, duck? I missed my breakfast this morning. I'm Clyde, by the way."

"Right, Clyde, do you take milk and is it one lump or two?"

"You couldn't make it four lumps, could you, duck? It's my blood sugar, you see."

Mollie didn't see, but went to brew up anyway. While she was waiting for the kettle to boil Jack entered the office. As usual he had spent the first ten minutes sitting on the toilet reading the racing page of his daily newspaper.

Now he confronted Clyde: "Can I help you?"

"Not really, duck. I'm here to remove your CCTV. You can show me the components though. Are they switched off?"

Mollie entered with the tea at this precise moment.

"Clyde, this is the supervisor, Mr Sugden. Jack, this is Clyde."

"You're not from Glasgow, are you, Clyde?"

Jack's attempted joke fell on cold porridge.

"No, duck, I'm from Stoke-on-Trent; now can you show me the gear?"

"I'll leave you in the capable hand of Mrs Knowles here – she is the administrator. I have to supervise outside, you see."

Jack turned and left without his usual cup of tea.

"Clyde, the camera is placed outside over the office door up by the roof; the rest of the apparatus is on that desk at the back of my office."

Clyde went to look at the inside unit.

"Oh, blimey, duck, this is out of the ark, this is."

"I'm not surprised, Clyde. You see, it's been here since the centre opened in the nineties."

"Well, duck—"

"I must stop you there, Clyde. I am neither a duck nor any other kind of avian species. I know that in this area the word 'duck' is a term of endearment, but I don't like it because, you see, last year I decided to serve duck for Christmas dinner. I went to the local supermarket and spoke to a member of staff: 'Do you have any duck?' I asked.

"The young woman replied, 'Yes, duck.'

"'Where is the duck,' I enquired.

"She answered, 'The duck, duck, is in the chiller cabinet.'

"I vowed then, Clyde, never to buy duck again or to use the word as a greeting. Now, what were you about to say?"

Clyde took a few seconds to get his head round Mollie's duck remarks.

"It's your system, d—, I mean, madam. You have the old analogue system, which has extensive wiring and physical connections to the recording device; however, it probably does allow multiplexing, unlike the more modern IP1080p HD-CCTV system's cameras, which capture images and audio and convert them directly into digital data which can be transmitted over the Internet network to remote recording devices like smartphones or Tablets. That system would allow you to view what is happening here in the compound from the comfort of your own home. Is your system switched off, by the way?"

"I believe so, Bonnie."

Clyde looked shell-shocked. "Why are you calling me Bonnie?"

"Surely you've heard of Bonnie and Clyde, the famous American bank robbers! They were shot dead, you know."

"I think I'd better make a start, duck."

"Good idea, Bonnie, but finish your tea first."

For the rest of the working day Mollie had to endure Clyde's presence as he went about his job. She soon found out that he had another annoying avian habit: he whistled constantly. Mollie mused that the cacophony might send her quackers, but she said nothing. Clyde finished half an hour before closing time.

"I'm ready to go now, duck. Oh, by the way, the system was still switched on."

"What happens to it now, Bonnie?"

"I've got to take it to the Environment Department at the council offices; I don't know what their plans are, duck. Bye. Thanks for the cuppas."

After he had left the compound, Jack came into the office.

"How did it go, Mollie?"

"He has removed it, Jack, but he told me the system was still switched on."

"That's my fault, Mollie – I never understand these modern devices – but never mind, there'll be nothing on the tape."

Jack would have said more, but some raised, angry voices caught both his and Mollie's attention; they looked out of the window and saw a three-against-one confrontation: Fred, Pete and Winston were all shouting insults at Dimitri.

"You'd better go and see what's up, Jack."

"Oh, they'll all calm down in a minute."

They didn't.

"Right, Jack, I'll go and see what the problem is; you stay here."

Mollie strode across the compound towards the warring males.

She heard Pete shout at Dimitri, "You're an interfering foreign twat, you are!"

Mollie attempted to calm the situation: "Gentlemen, please – this is no way to act."

Her plea fell on stony ground.

"Stay out of this, Mollie." Fred gave the order.

"Stay out of what?"

"None of your business, Mollie." Fred then turned to Pete and Winston: "Come on, lads, we'll discuss what to do in the pub."

The threesome turned and left Mollie and a very confused-looking Dimitri.

"Please can you tell me what they were on about, Dimitri?"

"I'll try, Mrs Knowles. Earlier today the small-electrical-items container was emptied as usual. Near the end of the process I saw a microwave oven stuck under the ramp; I lifted it out and gave it to the driver of the dumper. Just before closing time Fred came and looked under the ramp. I asked him what he was looking for. He told me a microwave, so then I told him what I had done and, as you say in English, he went ballistic. Then the other two joined in. I really don't understand."

"Neither do I, Dimitri, but Mr Sugden will have a word with them tomorrow."

"The centre is closed tomorrow, Mrs Knowles."

Of course he was right. Mollie left him with her cheeks aglow.

CHAPTER 11

Dr Julian Priest was about to enter the valley of death once again. He had parked his car near the front entrance of the Town End Care Home and prepared to enter the building.

Val Davies greeted him in the reception area: "Good morning, Doctor. Please sign in – Matron is waiting for you in her office. I'll bring two cups of coffee. Do you still have yours black?"

"Yes, please, Mrs Davies, with the usual surfeit of caffeine."

He found June Bailey at her desk looking pensive.

"Good morning, Matron. Well, here we are again – how many years is it now?"

"Twenty-three, Dr Priest."

"Ah yes, we were young and hopeful then – I wonder what went wrong."

June managed a wan smile as the Doctor opened his attaché case. "I'd like you to examine Miss Stones, Doctor."

"Has she got worse, Matron?"

"Definitely. She's very aggressive with women and sexually explicit with men. I've just hired a handsome young chap, and she's after him."

"You'd better accompany me, then, Matron, because I'm out of practice warding off ladies on heat. Life really is a stupid business, isn't it? I mean, if Miss Stones was fifty years younger she might get her wicked way and, if she became pregnant, she would have enough life expectancy to raise a family."

"Is she typical of a person with dementia, Doctor?"

"It's not unheard of, Matron. I suggest I prescribe some

strong sedatives – you could have some as well if you like."

"That's not a bad idea, especially with the turmoil I'm experiencing."

"Are you losing staff, then?"

"Everybody is fed up – no one has had a pay rise for years. I'm having to hire temporary, untrained people, many of whom are fly-by-nights. The local authority has cut its funding, and if I raise fees for residents who are financially independent I get lots of aggro from relatives. In short, it's a nightmare."

"People are living longer, Matron – mind you, I probably won't. Now, in addition to Miss Stones, I'd better have a look at Basil Weston; the last time I took his blood pressure it was in the stratosphere."

"He's still smoking, Doctor. He tries to hide the fact, but I have my spies."

"What about alcohol?"

"I have heard he has a season ticket at The Red Lion and he's become friendly with a young woman I've just hired as a cleaner."

"I see. Well, it sounds as though he's making a play for eternity. I'll have a word with him and point out the discipline required if he wants to stay on the planet, and I'll prescribe more statins. As I said earlier, we are living longer and I can't really see the point. None of us chose this life and we all face termination."

Fortunately the coffee arrived before Dr Priest became even more suicidal.

After finishing his coffee Dr Priest asked to see Basil Weston first – at least he was compos mentis and his libido seemed to be subdued, especially where men were concerned.

"Don't bother coming with me, Matron – I know the way."

He soon found room 18, but he paused by the door because he could hear voices inside the room. He waited for a few seconds before knocking.

"Come in, please." It was definitely Basil Weston's voice.

Inside Basil was sitting by the window and a young female was dusting the ledge.

"Good morning, Doctor. Good to see you again. This is Stacie, by the way – she cleans my room."

Dr Priest made a quick scan of the cleaner: she was thin and quick-moving.

"I've just finished, Doctor, so I'll leave you to it."

"You're new, aren't you?"

"That's right, Doctor; it's only my second week."

"She does a great job, Doctor. I'll see you tomorrow in the usual place, Stacie."

"Righto, Basil. Bye."

"So, Mr Weston, you have a girlfriend!"

"Oh, I just buy her a coffee now and then."

"And have a smoke perhaps? I could see she is a smoker, Mr Weston. Now I'm here to take your blood pressure."

"Is that really necessary?"

"Yes, definitely, because the last time I took it it was so high that if it was an event in the Olympic Games you would have won the gold medal. Hold out your left arm, please."

Basil felt the noose tightening around his left humerus; the pain was greater than he remembered from past examinations. The reason soon became clear.

"You are lucky to still be on the planet, Mr Weston. Now I'm being serious because you could have a stroke or a heart attack at any minute. You must give up smoking immediately and also moderate your alcohol intake – do you understand?"

"Yes, Doctor."

"If you want to become immortal carry on as you are. Now look, man, I've seen many elderly persons like yourself become vegetables in the blink of an eye; they can no longer communicate nor manage the basic human functions. Do you want to end up like them?"

"No, Doctor."

"Then you know what you must do. I can prescribe more statins, which, of course, will be a drain on the NHS, or you can show some self-discipline. Now I must see other patients. Goodbye."

Dr Priest made sure he had Matron accompanying him before he examined Miss Stones. Matron entered room 15 first.

"Dr Priest is here to see you, Miss Stones."

"Is it a man?"

"Yes, Miss Stones. You will remember Dr Priest, I am sure."

"Is he that tall, handsome chap?"

Matron was confused for a second or two by Ethel Stones' question, but then it struck her that perhaps the resident had come across Dimitri.

"Miss Stones, Dr Priest is here in his professional capacity: he needs to check your heartbeat and blood pressure."

Matron stepped to one side at this point to allow the Doctor to approach his patient; Ethel Stones scanned him from top to bottom.

"No, no, this is not the chap I need. I want that tall, dark chap who, I am sure, has everything in proportion."

Dr Priest tried to take the initiative: "He is not here at the moment, I'm afraid, Miss Stones, but if you will allow me to carry out a few tests I can report my findings to him."

This initiative seemed to be working.

"What tests, man?"

"Well, your heart rate for one – I will need to place my stethoscope on your chest."

The initiative continued to be functional.

"You mean my breast?"

"Yes, that is correct; now, can you open your blouse, please?"

"I've always had the most beautiful tits, as you can see."

Dr Priest did not rise to the bait; he placed the instrument in the appropriate place and gave an order: "Breathe normally, please."

"You men are all the same – cold-hearted – so I'm going to grab your balls."

The patient lunged forward; the Doctor almost jumped back. Matron intervened by grabbing Ethel's hand.

"Now now, Miss Stones, let us not get too frisky. Come, Doctor, I think your patient needs to calm down."

When they were outside the room Matron made a suggestion: "In future, Dr Priest, perhaps one of your female colleagues from the practice will be less tempting."

"I have been a GP for many years, Matron, but that was the first time my gonads have come into play. Who is the tall, dark person that Miss Stones mentioned? Is he a member of the medical profession?"

"No, Doctor, you are the only GP we have here; I think Miss Stones must have been referring to a young foreign chap I employ on a zero-hours contract from time to time, but now let me take you to see your other patients.

"Matron, I take it you have gone through all the necessary procedures before hiring this man and any other temporary staff."

"Doctor, at this present time I have to be creative – I need to save money whilst maintaining standards. The temporary staff I have hired have no real contact with patients, so I have not insisted that they have checks from the Criminal Records Bureau. I know I'm taking a risk, but needs must, as they say."

It was clear from Dr Priest's facial expression that he was not convinced Matron's ploy was appropriate, but he kept his doubts to himself.

Over at the borrowed bungalow Dave Pringle was fed up. He was both bored and scared. He knew he had to lie low because his former friends – those he had tricked out of money in London – would still be seeking him out and Dave knew how vicious they could be. He needed Denny to return to Bermondsey to reconnoitre the situation, but he had lost contact with him. Each day he phoned and texted and left voicemail messages without success. He even considered going to Manchester himself, but he had no idea where Denny would hang out.

Dave was even wary about walking into the small town where his grandmother's bungalow was situated. Would Denny do the dirty on him and reveal where he was hiding? He certainly might if there was enough cash offered, but Dave's saving grace was the stolen car parked in his grandmother's garage. Denny reckoned it was worth £20,000, so he was unlikely to sell Dave out for a few hundred; nevertheless the situation was worrying.

Today, to break his boredom, Dave switched on the television at lunchtime. Normally he paid little attention to the news, but today something caught his ear on the regional news broadcast. He heard that two bodies had been recovered from Salford Quays, but it was the departed's names that shocked

93

Dave into a near panic: Denny and his brother Reginald Mace were both dead. The announcer said that the cause of their deaths was unknown for the moment, but police were trying to contact their next of kin and their friends. Dave's panic increased: what if someone had acquired Denny's smartphone? Then they would have his own contact details. What if Denny had been murdered by former associates from London? Should Dave stay put or run? For the latter he would need cash urgently – there was the car, of course, but he was sure the police would still have it on their radar. He decided instead to force Stacie into some illegal fundraising from the care home urgently.

Fred, Pete and Winston had had a heated meeting in The Red Lion – so heated, in fact, that Syd Fawkes heard most of the argument. It was clear that all three had a massive grudge against a foreign colleague.

"The sooner that bleeder leaves the better." This was Pete Fenton's opinion, and the other two had agreed with him.

"Five hundred quid being sent for recycling – it makes you want to weep!" That had been Fred Urmston's evaluation of a situation that wasn't clear to Syd.

"We've got to come up with something else for Joey's next pickup."

The other two had agreed immediately with Winston Green.

Suddenly Fred had cottoned on to the fact that they were being overheard.

"Look, lads, let's sleep on it and discuss more ideas tomorrow."

He had nodded towards the bar; the others had understood the relevance of the gesture.

They finished their drinks and quickly left the pub.

Stacie arrived back at the bungalow just before 6 p.m. Dave made no effort to greet her because he was switching the television on.

"Hi, Dave. How—?"

"Shut up, Stacie – I need to watch the news."

Stacie could not recall a time in the past when her lover

needed to watch a newscast. She felt a question coming on, but kept her mouth shut. She sat down and observed Dave as he watched the broadcast. She could see he was very agitated – he even gave his full attention to the report from Westminster and then he sat through various foreign-news items in silence as though glued to the screen. Finally, towards the end of the slot, Stacie understood why he was in such a febrile state.

"Earlier today, at Salford Quays in Manchester, two dead bodies were recovered from the dock. Police have been able to identify them as brothers Dennis and Reginald Mace; both bodies have serious knife wounds and the men were probably murdered at the same time. Police are now trying to contact their families in the South London area. Police are also seeking help from anyone who may have seen or heard an argument in the Quays area within the last few days."

Dave switched the television off and turned to face Stacie.

"You know what this means, don't you?"

Stacie was not sure she knew the answer; actually she was not too upset that Denny had departed the scene, so she said nothing but merely raised her eyebrows.

Dave gave his answer: "It means that someone from London followed Denny up 'ere; they waited till he met his brother in Manchester, then they done both of them."

This time Stacie felt she had to comment: "You've no evidence that's what happened, Dave. It might have been a northern gang what killed them. Remember that Reg Mace was in prison in Manchester."

"They'll 'ave Denny's phone, Stacie, with all my details."

"Not necessarily, Dave; remember, he nicked it so it may have a load of details on it of God knows who."

"I can't take a chance, Stacie – we need to get out of 'ere."

"Where to, Dave?"

He slumped back in his chair; he had no idea. He knew he couldn't return to London because he now had no one who could check the situation for him – except Stacie, of course.

"Look, Stacie, you could return to the Smoke for a few days to find out what's what."

"Oh yes, and where do I stay? And who do I speak to?"

She was right, of course. Dave looked down at his feet.

Stacie attempted to help: "There's the car, Dave – Denny won't need it now, will he? We could go up to Scotland and flog it."

Dave thrust the idea through his limited intellect.

"Yes, there might be something in it: sell the car for 20,000 quid or so, stay up in Glasgow for a month or two then chance a return to London. They would need ready cash, of course. OK, Stacie, but we need some dosh, so we need to nick some things from the care home. Now listen: is it possible you could do a night shift because then you could let me in?"

"I don't know about a night shift, Dave, but I could probably let you in at the back door before I knock off one evening. You could hide in the laundry until most of the staff have signed out and all the residents are in bed – you'd have a long wait though."

Dave did not fancy the wait, but he knew he would be safe from any thugs in the care home and there could be rich pickings.

"When are you next on, Stacie?"

"I'll have to wait for a call, Dave, but they're very short of staff so it could be tomorrow."

Dave now felt more settled because they had the semblance of a plan.

Stacie tried to offer him more reassurance: "Look, Dave, if your former mates know where you are they'd have turned up before now."

Dave knew this to be true, but he was still worried about his future.

CHAPTER 12

The following day Mollie Knowles took an early call at The Tip.

"Good morning. Chelford recycling centre here. Can I help you?"

She recognised her caller's voice immediately – it was George Rampling.

"Is that Mrs Knowles, please?"

"Yes, Mr Rampling, it is."

"Good. Now, I've got some news and a question. The news is positive because I now have your former CCTV system. The engineer has told me it is still operable and therefore can be sold on despite its age; this, together with its other savings, may be worth £1,000 or so to the local authority. Of course, I've asked our Safeguarding Department to check it out, but I can't foresee any problem. Now, my question is this: has your supervisor made the necessary saving in staffing costs?"

"Yes, Mr Rampling, he has. Dimitri Rotarescu will leave at the end of the month. Mr Sugden hopes that the authority will pay him till his departure."

"Well, all right, Mrs Knowles, but this time only. You see, I've got some councillors and Tobias Argent on my back again. In fact I'm meeting Mr Argent later today and I've no doubt he will push for more staff changes. I'll let you know the outcome of the meeting in due course. Now, would you thank Mr Sugden on my behalf for his swift response to the cost-cutting exercise. Was there any trouble, by the way?"

"No, Mr Rampling, there wasn't. The choice of who should

leave was carried out in a democratic fashion and Mr Rotarescu has accepted the decision."

"Excellent, Mrs Knowles. Goodbye. I'll speak to you later."

As she replaced the receiver, Mollie mused that weak leadership could sometimes appear very effective.

Tobias Argent made sure he was ten minutes early for his meeting with George Rampling. He had asked Samantha Fagan to accompany him and he explained to her the reason for their early arrival.

"One of the things a successful politician must do is to keep the opposition off guard. Now, have you brought all your evidence with you, Miss Fagan?"

"Yes, I have, Mr Argent. Shall I produce the photographic evidence first?"

"Definitely, Miss Fagan."

The MP strode up to the main reception desk at the town hall and confronted the young woman on duty. She was short, dumpy and had a tattoo on the left side of her neck.

"I am here to meet Mr Rampling in the Environment Department. Inform him I'm here, will you?"

"Certainly, sir – one moment, please. The receptionist rubbed her nose before picking up a receiver. Her voice was so quiet that neither Tobias nor Samantha could hear the conversation, but within a few seconds she replaced the receiver and made eye contact with her MP.

"I'm sorry, sir, but Mr Rampling is on the telephone at the moment and you are a little early."

"Now, look here, young madam, you get on the phone again and inform him I'm on my way up."

"I'm not able to do that, sir – Mr Rampling has a very senior rank. I suggest you sit in this reception area until your appointed time; there's a coffee machine over by the window."

Tobias was having none of it: "Come on, Miss Fagan, we're going right now." As they waited for the lift Tobias voiced his political opinion: "You see, Miss Fagan, this is what is wrong with all public services – they are inflexible and they show no respect for authority. Don't you worry, I'll have Rampling off the phone in no time."

Samantha Fagan smiled at the politician while asking herself who was off guard now.

George Rampling's office was situated on the top floor of the town hall. Tobias knew which door to approach, but before he could announce himself his adversary appeared in the corridor.

"Good morning, Mr Argent. I hope you haven't been kept waiting." As he said this George looked at his wristwatch. "I believe you're smack on time – please come in. I'll ask Miss Shultz to make us some tea."

"I haven't got time for tea, man; I have to catch the one-o'clock train to Euston."

"Right-ho, so let's get down to business."

For the first time Tobias mentioned Samantha: "This is my new agent, Miss Fagan. She's carried out some important observations of goings-on at the Chelford recycling centre."

Tobias was surprised when George smiled at this juncture.

"I have some important information for you both as well, so please sit down."

Tobias was unaccustomed to lesser mortals taking the initiative, but he followed Samantha's lead and sat down.

"Well?"

George smiled again. "I have to report that my department has made substantial savings at Chelford. The site's CCTV has been removed – it is still in good working order and therefore can be sold on."

Tobias was not impressed: "Well, that's not enough, man."

"Indeed not, Mr Argent, but, in addition, one member of staff will leave at the end of the month. Now, surely these two savings should ensure that the facility can remain open with reduced staffing."

Tobias Argent paused before commenting because he had not expected that a member of the Chelford recycling-centre staff would leave so promptly. He realised that to keep his long-term plan alive he needed to keep the dust in the air, and of course he had Samantha's photographic evidence.

"You will no doubt remember, Mr Rampling, that when you and I, plus Councillor Nugent, made our inspection visit the Chelford recycling centre seemed very busy at an early hour; now, if you study the photographs taken by my agent here at the same time on other days, you will gain a very different opinion of business at the centre. And I believe Miss Fagan's research gives a much more realistic view. I shall, of course, share her research with other councillors, who I feel sure will agree that more savings can be made urgently. Now I have to leave because I have to travel to Westminster in an hour's time."

Tobias stood up to leave; Samantha joined him; George Rampling sat tight.

"Just one request, Mr Argent: could I have copies of your agent's evidence so I can show it to employees at the recycling centre? Such a ploy could well improve their understanding of the need for further savings."

Tobias reckoned he had won.

"Good idea, Mr Rampling." He turned to his agent: "See to it straight away, Miss Fagan, please."

George Rampling hoped he could return to other aspects of his job once the politician had left, but before he could switch on his computer he had a call on his internal phone. His caller was someone in the Safeguarding Department.

"Is that Mr Rampling?"

"Yes. Who is this?"

"Graham Snodgrass. I've been examining the tape from the CCTV at the Chelford recycling centre."

"Surely there's no problem, Mr Snodgrass?"

"Well, I don't know, but I think you need to take a look at the last images recorded because they cover a period after midnight a few days ago."

"Just tell me, please, Mr Snodgrass."

"Well, they show a truck and four blokes who load some large electrical goods, then the truck drives off but three of the guys return and place something in what looks like a microwave oven. Now, of course, I know nothing about recycling procedures, but it seems a strange time for genuine work."

George Rampling had to agree, although he did not admit it over the phone; instead he made a request: "Can I pop down to your department and have a look for myself, Mr Snodgrass?"

"No problem, Mr Rampling. I can even arrange a cup of tea."

Graham Snodgrass's colleagues called him the techno-geek behind his back. George Rampling found him staring at a screen with his spectacles pushed up to his forehead.

"Have a seat here, Mr Rampling. I'll run the footage through for you."

George found himself gazing at a grey screen with pretty-indistinct images.

"Sorry about the quality, Mr Rampling, but this system is really out of date now and of course the footage is at night."

Despite this George could make out a truck reversing into the compound.

"I can't make out the registration number Mr Snodgrass."

"Me neither, but one of these men must have a key to the main entrance."

George felt like saying, "I worked that one out too," but instead he gazed intently at the four persons in the footage. He was sure he'd seen a couple of them before, but he could not be 100 per cent certain. It was clear, however, that some dirty work was afoot. It suddenly struck George that if Tobias Argent got hold of the tape the Chelford recycling centre was doomed.

"Can you save this footage, Mr Snodgrass, so I can make further enquiries?"

The geek went into electronic mode.

"Of course, Mr Rampling, I'll save it on a USB stick, which I will give to you."

"Thank you, Mr Snodgrass. That will help my enquiries immensely, and we don't need to clutter the authority's system, do we, so could you delete it from there?"

"No problem, Mr Rampling." Graham Snodgrass tapped the side of his right nostril. "I'll have it in the computer system's recycling bin within two clicks."

'And I', thought George, 'will get to Chelford later today.'

Back in his own office George began to plan his next moves. First he decided to phone Mollie Knowles, as he had promised, to report on his meeting with Tobias Argent. During the course of the call he would tell her he needed to clear something up by visiting The Tip; he would say that he needed her opinion on the CCTV footage. Depending on her reactions, he hoped his next moves would be clear. He guessed she knew nothing about the robbery – would she be shocked? Would she insist Jack Sugden see the images or would she confess to knowing who was involved? George knew he was in a very difficult position – he ought to notify the police, but if he did that Argent would definitely find out and The Tip would be closed, which also would put his own job in jeopardy. He doubted he would find a similar position at fifty-five years of age. No, he must keep the robbery a secret, but he couldn't afford to let another theft happen – it was definitely time to visit The Tip.

Despite some worrying information from George Rampling, Mollie Knowles was having a relaxed afternoon. All her office work was up to date and there were very few persons recycling; in fact, three of the male workers were sitting on a ramp having a chat while Jack smoked a cigarette by the toilets and Dimitri was standing alone by the main entrance. He stepped aside as George Rampling drove into the compound. Mollie was surprised that Mr Rampling had insisted that he needed a visit in person. Quickly she switched on her computer and printer and she made sure she had a relevant document on the screen as she went to open the office door.

"Good afternoon, Mr Rampling. I was surprised when you told me earlier on the phone that you needed to visit us."

"Yes, I thought I'd come in person, Mrs Knowles, because, as I mentioned earlier, I have some very important and sensitive information. Please call Mr Sugden over."

Mollie was puzzled, but she stepped out of the Portakabin and shouted to Jack: "Mr Rampling needs to speak to you, Jack!"

The other workers all heard the summons. Pete Fenton, in particular, felt very perturbed.

He turned to Fred Urmston: "Eh, Fred, you don't think he knows about the other night, do you?"

"'Course not, Pete – keep your underwear dry."

Fortunately, at that precise moment two cars drove into the compound so Pete was not able to vent any more worries because he had to take up his normal position by the small-electrical-items container.

In the office Jack shared a similar set of concerns to Pete's. He was not expecting good news about the future and he wasn't about to be disappointed. When they were all seated George adopted a worried look.

"I met Tobias Argent earlier today and gave him the news about the savings we have managed to make at this facility."

Mollie and Jack felt optimistic at this point, but they both noticed that George still had a serious expression.

George's next contribution showed why: "Argent still believes we have to save more and he will pressurise local councillors; however, there is something even more worrying." George felt in a jacket pocket and produced the USB stick. "Please play this for us, Mrs Knowles."

Jack hadn't a clue what the device was, but he said nothing as Mollie inserted the stick into her computer. Three heads craned forward as the stored images showed on the screen.

Jack was first to react: "What the hell?"

Mollie had a clearer idea: "Hey, this shows The Tip, but whose is that truck?"

George also had a pertinent question: "Do either of you recognise any of the four men?"

Jack was sure he knew who three of them were, but it was time to fog the picture: "That slim one could be Dimitri."

Mollie disagreed: "Don't be daft, Jack! He's far too short and he's not broad enough either."

George uttered his next planned comment: "You will see at the top right of the screen that the footage is timed at ten minutes past midnight."

"Some blokes are nicking stuff."

This time Mollie could agree with Jack: "That's right and I know who three of them are."

Jack knew as well, but he continued to cast doubts: "You can't be sure it's Fred, Pete or Winston, Mollie – you can't see their faces properly. And who's the other guy?"

"I don't know who the other bloke is, but I've worked with Fred and Pete for a number of years." Mollie pointed at the screen. "Just look at that bloke's posture."

She was right, of course – Fred had had a curved spine since childhood.

"Are you going to notify the police, Mr Rampling?"

"I ought to, Mrs Knowles, but that would ensure the closure of this recycling centre and there would be job losses." He didn't include the phrase 'including mine'.

"So what will you do, sir?"

George turned to face Jack. "I despise Argent and all he stands for. I should notify the police, but we three would be soon out of work so I will report nothing. Fortunately, the only evidence of the theft is on this USB device. Now there must be no repeat of the robbery."

"How do we make sure, sir?"

"Right, Jack, first we confront your three colleagues with the evidence, then I point out that they could land up in prison. Obviously one of them has a key to the main entrance – he must give that back immediately, then all of them must promise that they will never again steal from here. If they do then I will reveal the evidence that we have just seen to the local police – I'll claim, of course, that it has just come into my possession from persons unknown. Right, Jack, call your three colleagues in here – let's see how they react."

"I'd better go to my recycling position when they enter, Mr Rampling."

"No, Jack, I want you here. There isn't a soul recycling anything at the moment; the foreign chap can stay outside."

It was clear Jack was very reluctant to carry out George's request, so Mollie stepped into the breach: "You stay here with Mr Rampling, Jack; I'll round up the gang."

The gang of three were highly suspicious when Mollie asked them to go to the office.

"Why the 'ell is Rampling 'ere again, Mollie?"

"He has something to show you all, and I'm certain you will all be amazed."

Reluctantly the threesome followed the administrator. Mollie left the Portakabin door open as they all squeezed into the office.

George took the lead: "Right, gentlemen, please make sure you can see the computer screen."

This request led to turning and shuffling movements similar to a popular television programme. After a few seconds George uttered his next order: "Right, Mrs Knowles, fire up the horror film."

George didn't look at the screen himself – his eyes were fixed on the audience. First he saw astonishment, followed by fear and then anger, particularly from Fred Urmston.

"Hey, what is this? It's nothing to do with anyone here." He looked at his two co-workers before adding, "Is it, lads?"

Pete and Winston immediately agreed with him, but George had planned for gang denial.

"So you'll all be quite happy when I show it to the local police?"

Each member of the gang lowered their heads.

"Do I take that as a no, then?"

Pete Fenton cracked first: "We only got rid of a couple of fridges."

"Even so you have all broken the law."

On hearing George Rampling's verdict, Winston made for the door; Jack Sugden's bulk prevented any escape, however.

George continued in his judicial role: "Now listen, you three: I have had a word with your bosses here and we have come to a joint decision. We will not notify anyone this time, but you must solemnly swear that you will not indulge in any more thefts, and whoever has a key to the main entrance must give it back. Do you all agree?"

This time three heads nodded in agreement.

The working day was over; Mollie found her coat and handbag before leaving the men. George Rampling followed her out of the Portakabin.

"Mrs Knowles, can I have a quick word before you leave?"

Mollie cursed inwardly, but she turned to face her superior. "I don't totally trust those three men; now, is there any way we can keep a check on them?" Mollie thought for a moment. "I could have a word with my friend at Harley Dumpers – its compound overlooks The Tip."

"Good idea! Please talk to him or her, Mrs Knowles, and let me know the outcome."

George was not the only person planning ahead. The gang of three had decamped to The Red Lion to discuss tactics. They were greeted warmly by Syd Fawkes because for the last two hours he had had only two customers – Basil Weston and Stacie were sitting at the window table dawdling over two coffees. Winston bought three half-pints of bitter and joined his colleagues at a table close to the bar's entrance.

Winston had taken the lead in initiating the session, but when they had all sipped their beer Fred opened the discussion: "Thanks for the drinks, Winston. What do you want to tell me and Pete?"

"My mate Joey, the Count, wants to arrange another pickup and he's offering 600 quid this time. Now—"

Pete butted in: "Impossible, Winston! Fred's given the key back."

Fred put him right: "I took a copy, Pete; in fact, I've got one for each of us."

Pete was still unhappy. "You 'eard what Rampling said about notifying the police."

Fred stared at his co-conspirator. "He was bluffing, Pete – there's no CCTV any more, and even if he did tell the cops he'd lose his job."

Winston attempted to support Fred: "Look, Pete, consider this: people bring their garbage voluntarily to The Tip, so who owns it? Remember, some is sold on so why can't we help the process? I mean, in a way we're entrepreneurs providing a useful service for the community. OK, we get paid, but that's only right, surely!"

Pete was confused by Winston's logic, so he offered no more questions or objections.

Winston continued: "I'll contact Joey later and arrange a collection, OK?"

"Two hundred quid each, you said, Winston?"

"That's right, Fred. Now drink up."

They had all spoken in low voices, but Syd Fawkes had caught the gist of their conversation. Earlier he had heard Stacie ask Basil about procedures at the care home.

"How many people are on duty at night, Basil?" she had asked.

He had said he wasn't sure, but he didn't think there were many.

"Do you think I could work on a night shift?" she had asked.

Basil had offered to find out for her.

Syd guessed that she was hoping for a better rate of pay for working unsocial hours; he didn't know her real reason, which was to help her partner, Dave, steal items from vulnerable elderly people.

CHAPTER 13

Mollie Knowles's first task the following day was to ring her friend at Harley Dumpers.

"Morning, Nora. How are you?"

"OK, Mollie – a bit fed up actually, but never mind. Now, what can I do for you?"

"We've had to make savings here at The Tip, Nora, and our CCTV has been dismantled. You've still got yours, I believe."

"That's right, Mollie. In fact, we've just had the latest model installed – it's the type you can access from a smartphone."

"Does it cover any of our compound, Nora?"

"Hang on a second, Mollie – I'll just check some of last night's footage." A few seconds later Nora gave her assessment; "Well, Mollie, it does cover your main entrance and a section of the driveway. What's the problem?"

"No real problem, Nora; it's just my big boss who wants to know. Does the new system cover all your own compound, then?"

"No, it doesn't, so the company has just hired a nightwatchman. Do you remember Johnny Cowan? He was in our year at school."

Mollie delved into her long-term memory.

"Was he that stringy lad who wanted to be a cricketer?"

"That's him, Mollie. He married that aggressive blonde who went to the grammar school. Anyway, he's survived. Would you like me to ask him to keep an eye on your place as well?"

"Yes, please, Nora. Tell him I'll buy him a drink sometime."

"Will do, Mollie. I must ring off – the boss has just arrived."

Over at Dave's grandmother's bungalow Stacie had received a welcome phone call from Matron at the care home: "Miss Holt, I have work for you today from midday till seven this evening. Can you attend, please?"

Stacie had been only too pleased to confirm her availability. Dave was also pleased, especially when Stacie told him that she would work into the evening.

"Right, I'll be in the backyard at seven; when the coast's clear let me in by the rear entrance."

"Dave there will be staff around at that time, so I'll have to hide you in the pressing room probably or the laundry."

"That's fine, Stacie. I'll wait till everything quietens down before having a shufti round the place."

"Remember, Dave, that the main reception area is covered by CCTV, but the backstairs aren't. If any of the night staff see you just say you're there on a zero-hours contract; no one will question it."

Dave's mood improved immediately the plan was agreed. Stacie, however, had a couple of doubts.

"You know, Dave, that most of the residents are off their heads and many are not mobile without help, but there are two who could cause problems. There's Basil Weston, for instance, in room 18. He's fully with it and he's given me support getting the job, so we don't want to upset him; and look out also for Ethel Stones in room 15. She's fully mobile and aggressive – you don't want to run into her. I'll go into town now and see if I can meet Basil so I can find out if there's anything special happening tonight."

"I'll come with you, Stacie – I'm fed up being stuck in here for hours."

"No, Dave, don't do that – the less Basil sees of you the better. I'll have a chat with him and a smoke and I'll report back to you here before I start my shift."

Stacie found Basil in his usual spot on the bench in Church Terrace.

"Hi there, Basil. How are you today?"

Basil puffed out a mouthful of smoke before looking up at her. "Oh, hi, Stacie. Yes, I'm OK today; how about you? Have you got any more work?"

"I shall be in the care home from midday till seven today, Basil. Unfortunately Matron has asked me to help in the kitchen with Ms Reeder."

"Oh dear! She's a right tyrant, isn't she?"

"She sure is, but at least I get paid."

"Do you help with the cooking?"

"I mainly do washing-up, but, even with that, Ms Reeder is watching all the time. Is there anything special on tonight, then, Basil?"

"No, I don't think so. Do you fancy a coffee in The Red Cat?"

"Yes, thank you."

Stacie watched as Basil hauled himself to his feet with a grunt.

"Are you OK, Basil?"

"Here's a piece of advice, Stacie: don't grow old. Can you please hang on to my arm till my left hip engages first gear?"

Slowly they made their way to the pub. Basil plonked himself down on the chair nearest the door before fumbling in his jacket pocket to find a banknote.

"Get us a couple of lattes, please, Stacie."

Stacie went to the bar to place the order. Syd Fawkes had noticed Basil's mobility problem.

"Is he OK?"

"Just his hip playing up, I think. I'll have a coffee with him and then offer to help him return to the care home."

Syd smiled at her. "That's good of you; I'd be upset if he lost his mobility."

When Stacie returned to the table Basil seemed to have perked up.

"You've heard about and seen enough of my problems, Stacie; now what about you? You've told me very little about yourself."

Stacie paused before answering – should she tell him the truth or improvise? She trusted him, so the truth it was.

"I was born in Bermondsey just over nineteen years ago;

Mum wasn't married and, in fact, I don't know who my father is. I doubt my mum knows either. She had problems, you see – drugs and that – and I was taken into care. I can remember a Mr and Mrs Cryer, but I must have been a big problem because I went into a home when I was five or six."

Basil interrupted at this point: "Well, Stacie, we have something in common, because we've both experienced care homes."

She smiled briefly before she added, "You went into one, Basil; I escaped from one. I was sleeping rough till I met Dave; he's looked after me since then."

"Where is he now, Stacie? I haven't seen him for days."

"He's thinking about our future together, Basil. His grandmother will return to Chelford soon and we'll have to move on. Have you finished your coffee, by the way?"

Basil had; Stacie drank the rest of hers in two gulps.

"Would you like some help getting back to the care home?"

"Yes, please, Stacie. Grab my left arm and I'll attempt to beat gravity."

Basil managed it slowly, and together he and his young friend made a wobbly exit from the pub. Syd watched them leave. He had overheard most of their conversation, and his conclusion was that he might soon lose two more regular customers.

Stacie left Basil by the care home's main entrance – he had assured her he could manage from there. She hurried back to the bungalow so she could inform Dave that she could let him into the home through the rear entrance. She wished she had a mobile phone because it would have saved her a walk.

She found Dave watching a twenty-four-hour news programme on television. Stacie paused before interrupting because she guessed – correctly, as it turned out – that her partner was seeking more information about Denny and his brother.

Finally Dave spoke while still keeping his eyes on the screen: "Have you spoken to old what's-'is-name?"

"Yes, Dave, I have, and he's told me that there's nothing special on at the care home tonight; so come with me and wait by the back entrance till the coast is clear. Then I'll let you in and put you somewhere safe – you can wait till the night shift is well under way before you come out. If you happen to bump into anyone pretend you're there as a temporary worker just for one night."

Dave was impressed by Stacie's planning, although he wasn't looking forward to a long wait in some hiding place.

The couple left the bungalow together, but separated near the main gate to the care home.

"I'll go in by the front door, Dave; you slip round the back and hide behind those big rubbish containers. Now, you may have to wait some time before I find you a hidey-hole."

Dave followed her instructions; he had brought some cigarettes, so he lit up while he waited. He had a fright about thirty minutes later when someone came to deposit food waste into one of the containers; fortunately it was not the one he had hidden behind.

Stacie went about her work as calmly as possible despite the fact that Ms Reeder was in a foul mood. Stacie was grateful that she had a co-worker, the very handsome Dimitri.

"I thought you were still at The Tip, Dimi."

"I had a call this afternoon asking me to help out tonight. The Tip is closed today."

By now two hours had passed and Dave's patience was like a piece of veneer that was about to peel off a main timber frame. He stubbed out his third cigarette and was just about to depart when Stacie finally arrived by the containers. She followed her nose and found him.

"Bloody 'ell, Stacie, where 'ave you been?"

"Keep your voice down, Dave. Now follow me – I'm going to put you in the pressing room because all today's laundry has been done. I've put a chair in there for you. Now you need to stay in there till it's late and the residents are all asleep; there are only two persons on duty so it should be dead easy searching the bedrooms."

Stacie did not mention that Dimitri was one of the staff on duty.

Within seconds Dave was safely ensconced in the pressing room. Stacie whispered her goodbye and left the care home –

her shift was over. Dave was faced with yet more boredom; he sat on the chair and lit another cigarette and waited till night was well established.

Winston, Fred and Pete had met at The Red Lion. It was Pete's turn to buy the drinks. Syd Fawkes was delighted.

"What's this, then, young Pete? Are you about to drink me dry?"

"No, Syd, we're just going to discuss things at work."

"Is there a problem, then?"

"No, not really at the moment. That foreign bloke has been kicked out, so that's a saving, but who knows what will happen in the future?"

Syd could understand Pete's concern because his own prospects were looking very bleak, so without another word he poured the drinks and put them on a tray.

"Don't pay me now, Pete – you may want some more a little later."

Pete frowned, but said nothing because he was concentrating on delivering the beers without a drop spilled. Syd stayed behind the bar with his ears open.

Once back at the table, Pete passed round the drinks and then sat with his back to the bar. He leaned forward; the other two did the same, so that when they spoke their voices were hushed.

Winston took the initiative: "Right, lads, I've been in touch with Joey. He can drive up here tomorrow night; he's willing to pay 800 quid for the right gear."

"Have you told him what's available?"

"Well, Fred, he wants to bring a mate who's an expert in appliances so he can choose the best."

Pete wanted more information: "What's 'is mate called, Winston?"

"Cuthbert."

"Cuthbert?"

"That's right, Pete, but don't think he's a softy because he ain't; he's a big ex-boxer and he likes to be called Cutty."

"You mean like Cutty Sark?"

"He's almost as big as a ship, Fred – not a bloke to be messed about with, I can tell you. He'll be great at loading stuff on to the truck though."

Winston's co-conspirators were satisfied, so Fred sought confirmation of the pickup arrangements: "So we do the same as last time, then, Winston?"

"Definitely, Fred, and this time we don't 'ave to worry about CCTV, do we?"

The other two laughed and drank up.

"You're not going so soon, are you, lads?"

Fred answered the barman: "Sorry, Syd, but it's time to return to our happy homes. Pete, you pay the man."

After they had left, Syd mused on the little he had overheard – something to do with Cutty and a pickup. Now, what the hell was going on? Should he mention it to Jack Sugden? he wondered.

CHAPTER 14

Dave was now convinced it was safe for him to leave his hiding place. He had felt claustrophobic in the pressing room – so much so that he had indulged in two more cigarettes to help lessen his feeling of confinement. This caused a problem because he could not see anywhere where he could ditch the burnt cigarette ends. After several minutes of thought he decided to try the room next door – the laundry. At first he was stumped but then he decided to toss the ends into a washing machine – surely no one would find them there! He took a deep breath and made for the backstairs, taking a small torch from his pocket as he did so.

The first-floor corridor was dimly lit and the only noises were snoring sounds coming from the various rooms. Dave examined each door in turn, trying to find one that wasn't completely shut. He had no luck until he came to room 15. The door was ajar. Dave pushed gently and received the shock of his life because standing before him, in the half-light, was a white wraithlike figure which stretched out a hand towards him. Should he run for it or kick out?

He did neither because the phantom spoke in a clear aggressive voice: "You, man, get me a glass of water now!"

Dave stepped back, but the figure advanced and thrust a glass tumbler at him.

"Come on, man, do it now and make sure you have left it in my room by the time I return from the toilet."

The figure pushed past him with a rustle of almost luminous lingerie. Dave turned and watched the wraith stride down the corridor. This was a clear opportunity and Dave took it: he entered the room, switched on his torch and flashed it around. He saw a set of drawers. Quickly he made his way across the floor. He opened the top drawer and shone his torch in. Something sparkled back at him. He grabbed it, closed the drawer and made a fast exit. This was no time to examine his booty, especially as he heard a toilet flush somewhere along the corridor.

He sped back to the pressing room, where he took some time to examine the jewellery. In his hand he had a pearl-and-silver necklace. He smiled, but did not hang around – it was time to leave.

The wraith returned to her room.

There was no water and she flew into a rage: "Men are so damned useless!" she shouted loudly.

It was after midnight when Dave arrived back at the bungalow; everything was in darkness and silence reigned. Dave made his way to the rear bedroom, which he shared with Stacie. As he approached he heard deep regular breathing, but this was no time to let sleeping girls lie. He switched on the main light; still Stacie slept on. Dave went to the bed and gently shook her shoulder; she awoke with a jerk.

"What the—?"

"It's only me, Stacie. Look at this." Dave fished the necklace from his pocket and dangled it before Stacie's face.

"Where did you—?"

"In the care home, of course. This old bird asked me to get her a glass of water while she went to the bog, so I nipped into her room and found this in her top drawer. It's a real pearl necklace and I bet it's worth a mint."

Stacie was also impressed by the acquisition, but she had a couple of niggly doubts.

"Which room did you find it in, Dave?"

"Oh, I don't know – it was on the first floor near the toilets."

"The old bird you mentioned – who was she?"

"I don't bloody well know, do I? She looked like a ghost."

"So she was fully mobile and aggressive?"

"Look, Stacie, none of this matters – I've got us something

valuable and when we get to Scotland we can flog it."

Stacie asked no more questions, but her worries remained. She had no doubt that Dave had encountered Ethel Stones; the positive thing was that Miss Stones had mistaken Dave for an unknown member of staff. Would she recognise him again and how much stink would she raise when she found out her necklace was missing?

"We must do it again, Stacie. Try and get work on the same shift."

There was something else of which neither Stacie nor her lover was aware: another resident had had a fleeting glance of Dave as he made his escape from room 15 and that someone was Basil Weston.

Johnny Cowan was really happy in his new job. He clocked in at 10 p.m. and then spent ten hours in relative comfort. He kept his eye on the CCTV screens from time to time while he had cups of tea, and every hour he strolled round the compound to examine those areas where the CCTV system was blocked by machinery. If it was raining Johnny changed the system to two-hour intervals. He always had his smartphone with him, on which he could connect with the Internet.

Johnny had had many jobs during his working life, and most of them were either totally boring or knackering or both, but here at Harley Dumpers there was no one watching his every move. Tonight he was feeling very relaxed – so much so that he felt his eyelids close from time to time as he lolled in Nora Stubbins' chair. He remembered his past triumphs in the local cricket league: the day he had scored thirty-four not out for Chelford Second Team against close rivals Leek Over-Fifties and the time when he had downed two pints in ten seconds after a match in the Trent Valley. His memories assumed a dreamlike state. Suddenly voices and a mechanical noise brought him back to full consciousness. He gazed at the screen in front of him: someone was reversing a truck into the Chelford recycling centre. It was a tight fit and the voices were obviously giving the driver directions. Johnny glanced at his watch; it was after midnight. Surely the recycling centre wasn't open this late! His CCTV system did not cover the whole area of the recycling centre's compound – Johnny could see the front part of the truck only; the driver was indistinct. He assumed it was some special arrangement, so he tried to return to his former soporific state. He couldn't because there were now metallic clanging sounds and more loud voices. He guessed the truck was being loaded. He decided to take some snaps with his smartphone. As he did so a man came into view; he staggered and fell to the ground, then another figure appeared being chased by a giant wielding what looked like a metal stave. Both of these men disappeared from sight, but then the giant returned alone and Johnny saw three men climb into the truck and drive off into the night. The first figure remained motionless on the ground and Johnny knew he must ring 999.

Jack Sugden was fast asleep when his landline phone rang. It didn't wake him up, but it did his wife, Corin. Corin's angry voice soon woke him up.

"What do you mean he needs to go to The Tip now? It's after one o'clock. I don't care if there's trouble – he's staying here."

Jack's brain crawled into action.

"Who is it, dear?"

"It's the police. They say there's trouble at The Tip. They want you there now because you're a keyholder."

Jack held out his hand: "I'd better speak to them. Who is this, please?"

The voice at the other end sounded tinny and decisive: "PC Winsford of the local police here, Mr Sugden. There's been a robbery at the recycling centre and we need you here because there's some CCTV footage."

"That can't be correct, Constable – our CCTV has been removed."

"Not yours, Mr Sugden, but the new system at Harley Dumpers, and we've got a witness – the nightwatchman."

"I'm on my way, Constable."

Corin had overheard the conversation.

"I'd better drive you, Jack, because you had quite a lot to drink earlier."

There was very little traffic on their way to The Tip, but

suddenly two ambulances appeared rushing towards them.

"I wonder if they're anything to do with the trouble, Jack?"

"I don't know, Corin, but we're going to find out pretty soon because we're almost there."

Corin turned on to the driveway that led to The Tip, but she had to pull up short because a police car was blocking the way. Jack noticed three figures in the darkness: two were obviously policemen; the other was unknown to him. One policeman came towards him as he left the car.

"Are you Mr Sugden?"

"Yes, officer. What's happened, please?"

"Well, we could be looking at a robbery with actual bodily harm. Now, I'd like you to accompany me and Mr Cowan over there – he's nightwatchman at Harley Dumpers and he's got something relevant on that firm's CCTV."

While Jack accompanied the copper and Johnny up the hill, Corin spoke to the other policeman: "Are you sure it's a robbery, officer?"

This policeman was young and slender – he might even have been a trainee, but nevertheless he answered Corin's question: "PC Winsford is not sure because there's no sign of a break-in."

Corin asked nothing else because she suspected that Fred Urmston probably still had a key to the main entrance.

Jack was now scanning the CCTV footage. He saw the body fall to the ground and at once he recognised Fred Urmston; then he saw Pete Fenton being chased out of shot.

PC Winsford turned to Johnny: "You said earlier that you've taken some pictures on your smartphone."

"Yes, I did, but they've not come out well – obviously it was too dark."

The officer turned back to Jack: "Do you recognise anyone on the CCTV, Mr Sugden?"

Jack desperately needed time to think. It was quite clear to him that Fred and Pete were up to their tricks again; but if he identified them The Tip would close, so he attempted a delaying tactic.

"I'm not sure, officer. Could my wife join us? She might be able to help."

The ploy worked.

PC Winsford contacted his young colleague: "Ben, please ask Mrs Sugden to join us at Harley Dumpers; you stay there and tape off the entrance."

While they waited for Corin to join them Jack enquired about the ambulances he'd seen earlier: "Did the person seen on the CCTV need hospital treatment, officer? I saw a couple of ambulances as I drove here."

"The person we have just seen being chased has a very serious head injury. He went in the first ambulance. The other chap probably has concussion and possibly a broken arm. I'll speak to him later at the hospital."

Corin joined the men.

Jack made sure he explained the need for her help first: "Right, Corin, the officer wants you to view the CCTV footage to see if you recognise anyone. I've had a go and I can't be certain."

Jack made sure he was staring into his wife's eyes as he said this.

She gazed at the footage and then shocked Jack: "Yes, officer, I have recognised both Fred Urmston and Pete Fenton."

"You're definite about that, are you, Mrs Sugden?"

"Yes, and I believe I know what has happened."

Jack tried to interrupt her: "Surely not, Corin! I mean—"

Corin cut him short: "There was a robbery taking place, officer. Fred and Pete saw what was happening and tried to intervene – that's why they were attacked. And there's something else because, as the truck drove off, there were three men in the cab and I bet one of them was Winston Green, who's been working at The Tip. You need to stop that truck before it gets to its destination."

"Where do you think would that be, Mrs Sugden?"

"Well, officer, Winston Green comes from South London, so my guess is that is where they're heading. Now you need to cut them off on the motorway system as soon as possible."

"Thank you, Mrs Sugden – your idea is certainly worth pursuing. I'll contact the station immediately."

PC Winsford left them, and soon they heard him talking, presumably to a superior officer.

Corin grabbed her husband's arm: "Come on, Jack, let's get back to our car."

Johnny Cowans was left alone at last. He needed a strong cup of tea.

Once outside, a family feud erupted: "Corin, what the hell do you think you're doing?"

"Saving your flipping job, Jack. Now look, we've got to get to Fred before the cops do."

"Why, Corin?"

"Jack, you and I know that he and Pete were in on the robbery. Obviously there was an argument – probably about money. Things got nasty and they were attacked. If the police prove their involvement, they'll go to prison and the council have a great opportunity to close The Tip; they could even try to implicate you in the theft."

Jack's mouth fell open because he hadn't considered he might be implicated.

His wife continued: "The story is this: Fred and Pete were spending time together when Fred remembered he'd left something at The Tip; he and Pete went to retrieve it and discovered the robbery taking place; they tried to intervene, hence the fight. Have you got that, Jack?"

Jack merely nodded his acceptance.

"When we get home, Jack, ring the hospital straight away and find out when we can visit Fred."

Fred Urmston was divorced, he had no children and both his parents were dead. Corin explained this to the ward sister on the phone after she and Jack had arrived home. "My husband and I are close friends of his, you see, Sister, and we would be very grateful if we could visit him early tomorrow to do our bit in helping him recover."

The Sister agreed to this request: "Five minutes maximum, Mrs Sugden, at nine o'clock."

Corin could gain no information about Pete because he had had to be moved to a specialist unit.

Next morning at eight o'clock Jack had a call from the local police: "We need an early meeting at the recycling centre,

Mr Sugden, to establish what has been stolen. You keep an inventory, I take it."

"I'm sure my colleague Mrs Knowles, who is the administrator, will have comprehensive data, officer."

"Good! Now a Mr Rampling will join us as well."

Jack was now feeling fragile – it was time to involve Mollie Knowles.

Corin arrived at the hospital reception a few minutes late because she had had difficulty finding a parking space. It took her some more time to discover which ward Fred was in, but at last she appeared at the ward entrance and managed to convince the nurses on duty that she had been given permission to speak to him.

"The night sister said I could have five minutes alone with Mr Urmston."

"He's at the back of the ward on the left-hand side."

Corin thanked the young nurse and hurried over to where Fred was lying. His head was swathed in bandages and his left arm was in plaster, but at least he was conscious.

"I've got to get out of here, Corin."

"Now, hang on, Fred – you've been badly injured."

"The police will be after me, Corin."

Corin felt relieved because it was clear the police had not been to question him yet.

Corin lowered her voice: "Don't fret, Fred, just listen. Jack and I have already spoken to the cops and we've told them that you and Pete almost certainly came across the robbery accidentally as it was being carried out, so you attempted to stop it but you were attacked by the thieves. Jack and I know you and Pete were actually part of the gang, but we've been trying to save both your skins."

"But why were we at The Tip at that time, Corin?"

"You and Pete spent the evening together at his place and then you remembered you'd left something at work; you went to fetch it and Pete accompanied you. Now you've got to decide what you had left at The Tip – can you manage that, Fred?"

"I must have left my overcoat and of course I have a spare key."

"I thought you had had to relinquish your spare key, Fred."

"I gave one to George Rampling, but then I found I had a second at home; I was going to give it in today actually."

"Well done, Fred. If you stick to this story you and Pete could become heroes."

Corin noted a doubtful look come into the one eye that was visible on Fred's face.

"Pete will have to say the same as me, Corin – are you going to see him now?"

"I'm sorry to tell you this, Fred, but Pete has had to be moved to a specialist unit. He's very badly injured, obviously."

Corin was about to add more, but a nurse, accompanied by a uniformed policeman, appeared at the bedside. Corin said farewell and mentally crossed her fingers.

Corin had the car, so Jack had to walk to The Tip. There he found a policeman guarding the gate, but he let Jack enter. Jack went straight to the office, where he found two more coppers and an annoyed Mollie Knowles.

Mollie announced his entrance: "Sergeant Locke, this is Mr Sugden, the supervisor."

There was no sign yet of George Rampling; Sergeant Locke, however, was not inclined to hang about.

"I have some good news for you, Mr Sugden: two men have been arrested at Warwick Services on the M40; their truck had various white goods very similar to those shown on the CCTV footage. Of course we have to verify that the items were stolen from here."

Mollie posed a question: "Can you tell us the names of the men you've arrested, Sergeant?"

"Yes, there's Joseph Miller and Cuthbert Wrench. Their truck was stolen from a firm in South London some time ago, so we can definitely hold them on that charge."

"But on the CCTV there was a third individual."

"That is correct, and we're trying to find him as I speak. Can you help us at all?"

Mollie decided she could: "Mr Sugden and I believe it is Winston Green, who has been working here at The Tip."

The Sergeant turned to Jack: "Is that correct, Mr Sugden?"

"I believe so, officer, and it's worth noting that Winston comes from South London."

"Right, I'll contact the team at Warwick Services and ask them to search for this man. They'll need a photograph, of course – do you have one here?"

Mollie assured him that she had one stored.

"Good. I'll send it to my colleagues, then I need some details of the stolen items. Do you have reference numbers, by any chance?"

Jack needed to point out how the recycling worked: "Sergeant, we have tons of stuff coming through the centre; it's quite impossible for us to keep track of every microwave oven, mattress or kettle."

"I understand that, Mr Sugden, but, as you know from the CCTV pictures, some items on the truck were very large."

Mollie attempted to help out the Supervisor: "The larger items would have been stored in the shipping container, Jack. Sometimes when people bring large items, they seek advice as to where they should leave them; I always tell them to deposit them in the parking area so that you and other staff can move them later to the former shipping container. Now, if such items look to be of recent manufacture, and are undamaged, I do take photographs and record other details – like serial numbers, for instance."

The Sergeant was delighted.

"Excellent, Mrs Knowles! Now let's examine this shipping container."

It was obvious from his first glance into the container that Jack knew several items had been taken; in particular he remembered a large American-style fridge-freezer that had been brought in a couple of weeks ago. Mollie even remembered who'd deposited it because a smart elderly chap had called in at the office; he had explained that he was moving into the smartest road in Chelford and he wanted to furnish his new residence in a style that suited him and his wife. Mollie had pointed out that the item would be worth selling, but he had explained that he needed all the space in the new house immediately. It took only a quick phone call from Sergeant Locke to confirm that the fridge-freezer now at Warwick Services had the same serial number as the one Mollie had recorded. Everyone present was delighted, as was George Rampling when he finally arrived. The one remaining mystery was the whereabouts of Winston Green.

"When can the recycling centre reopen, Sergeant?" George posed the question after he had absorbed the facts.

"I'm sure tomorrow will be fine, Mr Rampling, but I'd better check with my boss."

Jack had a problem with the timing of the proposed reopening; he turned to George Rampling: "I don't have enough staff to open tomorrow, Mr Rampling; Pete Fenton is in a bad way and Fred Urmston has a broken arm."

"But you've still got that foreign bloke, haven't you?"

"Yes, till the end of the month, but right now there are just two men – me and Dimitri. And Mrs Knowles, of course," Jack added quickly.

George Rampling turned to Mollie: "Mrs Knowles, could you—?"

Mollie knew what was coming so she cut him off: "Mr Rampling, I am employed as the administrator – I shall certainly not work outside. And may I remind you that it is from my record keeping that we have solved this crime. I suggest you speak to Dimitri Rotarescu and ask him two things: one, will he stay on here and, two, does he know of anybody seeking work?" She almost added, "Perhaps you could put in a shift or two?" But she restrained herself.

George beat a retreat after agreeing that Jack should follow up Mollie's questions.

Later in the day two more visitors turned up unannounced. Mollie heard someone knocking on the Portakabin door; she expected the police, but when she opened up she confronted two women, one of whom seemed familiar.

"Mrs Knowles, is it?"

Mollie nodded.

"I'm Samantha Fagan and this is Paula Gell."

"How can I help you ladies?"

Samantha took the lead again: "I'm the political agent for Tobias Argent, our local MP. He has heard about the robbery here and he is keen for our local newspaper to report the facts. This is Paula Gell. She is a reporter for the *Moorland Observer*. She would like to interview you and anyone else in the know."

Mollie remembered the advice given to her by her father years ago: always make a record of what you say to the press.

"I'll just get my supervisor, Samantha. Please wait here."

Jack joined the three women very reluctantly after Mollie had explained why his presence was important.

"I'll take notes of the questions and our replies, Jack."

Once again Jack found himself trapped in an enclosed space under pressure.

Paula Gell started the questioning: "What do both of you know about this robbery?"

Jack felt he could answer this one. He explained how he had had a call from the police to which he had reacted urgently. He described how he had viewed the CCTV footage together with his wife and how they had both recognised Fred Urmston.

Mollie now intervened: "Mr Sugden's wife visited Mr Urmston earlier today in hospital and he was fit enough to explain how he came to be attacked."

Jack realised that he must take over, so told the reporter the made-up story.

After hearing the concocted facts, Samantha Fagan had a question: "What about his friend, Mr Fenton?"

Jack hesitated; Mollie didn't: "He's very seriously injured and has been moved to a specialist unit, hasn't he, Jack?"

"Yes, that's right."

Mollie expanded on the robbery's outcome: "The police agree with us that both men are heroes; we all have no doubt that they prevented an even more serious robbery."

"Will this recycling centre have to close down now?"

Mollie stared at the reporter. "No, the police say we can open tomorrow – that's correct, isn't it, Mr Sugden?"

"Definitely, Mollie."

Samantha tried another track: "I have heard that the centre here is under threat of closure; is that true?"

Before answering, Mollie made a mental note that Samantha was recording everything on her smartphone. The situation called for leadership.

Mollie stared at the politician's agent. "No, that is not true – we have made considerable savings. Mr Sugden here has led the way by making important decisions which everyone now accepts. We have dispensed with excess bureaucracy and we have modified our staffing structure."

"But, surely, with the injuries, you will not be able to cope?"

Mollie continued her stare. "We have a flexible staffing structure, Miss Fagan, and we will open tomorrow, won't we, Mr Sugden?"

Jack had his doubts, but he needed to back up Mollie's assertion: "Definitely, and now you must excuse me so I can make the necessary arrangements."

The meeting was over and the interrogators left.

"Mollie, we need to speak to Dimitri pronto."

CHAPTER 15

Syd Fawkes was studying The Red Lion's balance sheet when two new customers entered the bar.

"Good afternoon, gentlemen. Now, what can I get you?"

"I wonder if you can 'elp us, mate? We're looking for our friend – he's called Dave Pringle. We've 'eard he's up 'ere with 'is partner."

Syd's potential customer was tall, unshaven but smartly dressed. Syd recognised a London accent.

His companion, who was shorter in stature but clean-shaven and boasting a striking tattoo of a snake on the left side of his neck, now entered the inquiry: "She's called Stacie."

Syd played for time and profit: "Right, I'll have a think. Would you like a drink, by the way?"

The taller guy recognised Syd's profit motive: "OK, mate, we'll 'ave two pints of bitter – now can you 'elp us?"

"Well, I get a lot of customers in here, you know, so could you give me a description of either or both of your friends?"

To Syd's surprise the shorter of the two Londoners took over: "Dave Pringle is a dark-haired, spotty berk and his bird is a thin-lipped twat with 'ardly any tits."

Syd pretended he was considering the descriptions. He had recognised both Dave and Stacie despite the colourful language, but he was wary of the shorter guy's aggressive manner.

"No – sorry, lads – I've never seen either of them in here. Right, I'll pull your pints."

The promise of alcohol did nothing to quell the short guy's frustration: "No, mate, keep it in your bleedin' bladder."

Syd watched as they left the bar together. He decided he must at least let Stacie know that someone was trying to find her.

Syd's problem was partially solved later in the afternoon when Basil arrived in the bar.

"Hey, Basil, where's your bit of stuff today?"

"Don't know, Syd – why do you ask?"

"Oh, a couple of guys were in here earlier looking for her and her boyfriend."

"Did they say who they were and what they wanted, Syd?"

"No, Basil, they didn't, and one of them was a nasty little creep – very aggressive. Young Stacie needs to be warned."

"I might see her later today, Syd. What did they look like?"

"Well, they're both definitely from the South – I could tell by their accents – and the shorter one had a tattoo on his neck."

"On his neck?"

"Yeah, a gold-and-black serpent. You can't miss it."

"And they didn't say what they wanted?"

"No, but they were definitely unfriendly. Would you describe a female friend as a twat with no figure?"

"Right, Syd, I'll let her know. Now I'll have my usual, please,"

Stacie had had a call from the care home. Val Davies told her the cook had requested her presence from midday till 7 p.m. Stacie had immediately agreed, despite the fact she would come under orders from Maggie Reeder; she hoped Dimitri would join her in the kitchen. After the call she went to find Dave. He was in the garage with his head in the engine compartment of the BMW.

"Dave, I've got more work today at the care home on the same shift as last time."

Dave's head appeared from the inner workings; he had a dirty smear on his right cheek.

"Good, Stacie – we'll do the same as last time."

Stacie was curious; she knew Dave liked cars, but in her experience he had only admired the external appearance, never the inner workings.

"What are you doing to the car, Dave?"

"I was just checking everything is in place. It's a great vehicle – it's definitely worth thousands. Now, I'll come to the care home just before you knock off; you'll find me behind the rubbish bins."

"Can you get your own lunch today, Dave? I've got to leave for work soon."

"No problem, Stacie."

When she had left, Dave decided he would venture into town and buy some sandwiches and a can of Coke from the local supermarket. It was a fine day, so Dave decided to eat his lunch outdoors. After making his purchases, he walked to Church Terrace and sat on one of the benches. He was into his second sandwich when he became aware that someone had sat down on the other bench. He looked over and saw Basil Weston, who, as always, had lit a cigarette after eating lunch at the care home. Neither male made any effort to make eye contact: Dave continued chewing, Basil puffing.

It was when Basil had nearly finished his smoke that he remembered his conversation with Syd Fawkes; he wondered whether he should mention the fact that two men were asking after Stacie. He decided not to bother because this Dave was unfriendly; no, Basil would wait till he met Stacie on her own.

He threw his cigarette butt to the ground, stamped on it and left. Dave made no reaction – he stared straight ahead and continued chewing.

Later, at five minutes to seven, Stacie left the kitchen with Maggie Reeder's permission. She found Dave smoking behind the rubbish bins and gave him the all-clear; she then left him and entered the care home again to find her coat. Dave had decided that he would not wait so long on this occasion as he had the first time, because he reckoned that by 9 p.m. everything would have settled down. He stayed in the laundry room for almost two hours before venturing forth.

He used the backstairs and was about to enter the first floor when loud screaming stopped him in his tracks. From the top of the stairwell he could watch developments without being seen. He saw a member of staff rush into room 15 and then he heard raised voices; another staff member arrived at the room, then the ghost Dave had seen on his last visit appeared almost pulling a nurse with her.

"Someone has stolen my necklace!" she yelled.

The Nurse tried to calm her, to no avail, and now the ghost saw the male staff member.

"It's him that's done it!" she wailed.

Dimitri was her target. He stepped back.

"Done what?" he asked.

The ghost was now sobbing loudly – the Nurse helped her back into the bedroom.

Shortly afterwards she reappeared and spoke to Dimitri: "Call the police, please, Dimitri. Their presence might help to calm her down."

Dimitri left the floor and was closely followed by Basil Weston from room 18, who wanted to know what all the fuss was about.

Everything went quiet. Dave tiptoed quickly to Basil's room – he had remembered that Stacie had told him that Basil had some valuable medals in a brass box. He found the box on the window ledge. Quietly and quickly he took the medals out and replaced them with three coins – a fifty-pence piece and two pennies – then he turned and made his exit. He reckoned that, by leaving the coins, anyone who picked up the brass box – a cleaner, for example – would not be made suspicious.

Stacie was in bed when Dave returned to the bungalow. He had decided he wouldn't tell her about his latest acquisitions because she might just get stroppy, so he hid the medals in a sideboard drawer in the lounge. Stacie was still awake when he entered the bedroom.

"You're early tonight, Dave. Did you get anything?"

"No, love. Some old dear started yelling, so I decided to leave, but there'll be other times."

PC Winsford, who was on duty at Chelford Police Station, took Dimitri's call.

"A stolen necklace, you say? And do you have any idea how much it's worth?"

"Miss Stones says it's worth hundreds of pounds."

"I see. Unfortunately I don't have any staff available at the moment, so please tell the lady someone will come tomorrow – probably in the morning – to make a full examination."

Dimitri went back to room 15 with the news. Surprisingly he found Miss Stones asleep.

"I've given her a sedative – she needs to rest," the Nurse told him.

Dimitri couldn't agree more: "Good, because the police can't do anything till tomorrow."

Next morning Dimitri arrived at The Tip at his usual time, ten minutes before opening time. To his surprise he found Jack Sugden waiting to talk to him.

"Good morning, Dimitri. I've got some good news for you: George Rampling would like you to stay on working here. You probably know that both Fred and Pete were injured in the robbery."

"Will there be just the two of us, Mr Sugden?"

"Well, Mollie is still here, of course, but outside in the compound there'll be just me and you, which reminds me that Mr Rampling is keen for us to hire another worker. Do you know of anyone? Someone at your hostel perhaps?"

"Could a girl be employed here, Mr Sugden?"

"Well, yes, I suppose so if there's no man available."

"OK, I do know someone who may be interested. I'll ask her later today."

Jack wanted more details, but was prevented from asking for them because it was now opening time. Dimitri opened the main gate, but there were no customers waiting. Jack took the opportunity to speak to Mollie about the staffing position. He found her sitting by her desk reading a newspaper. She looked up as Jack entered with a bemused expression on her face.

"Have you seen today's *Moorland Observer*, Jack?"

"No – anything interesting in it, Mollie?"

"We are in it, Jack, all over the front page."

"Could you read it out to me, Mollie? I haven't got my reading glasses."

"OK, but you'd better sit down."

Jack sat beside her. He was able to read the headline without spectacles: 'HEROES OF THE TIP'.

Mollie took a deep breath and read on: "Two heroic workers, employed at Chelford Town Recycling Centre, interrupted a robbery on Wednesday night. Fred Urmston and Pete Fenton happened to be passing the recycling centre when they saw the robbery taking place. Both men intervened to stop the theft and both were injured in the fight that ensued. Their heroic action delayed the thieves so that police were able, shortly afterwards, to identify their vehicle, and later Warwickshire Police made two arrests at Warwick Services on the M40. Unfortunately the two heroes both needed emergency treatment and both remain in hospital, with Mr Fenton possibly suffering life-changing injuries.

"The local Member of Parliament, Tobias Argent, was quick to praise the men. 'Theirs was a courageous act that shows the devotion that our council workers have for local services. Chelford Town Recycling Centre is an important local facility that carries out essential tasks for the whole community; it is efficient and highly cost-effective. I, personally, will do my utmost to support the injured heroes.'"

Mollie raised her eyes from the newspaper and looked across at Jack Sugden; almost at once they both burst into laughter. As Mollie said later to her friend Nora Stubbins, it was either laughter or the total use of every four-letter expletive in the English language.

WPC Olive Winsford was not looking forward to interviewing Ethel Stones at the Town End Care Home. Olive had undertaken similar tasks at the home in the recent past, questioning muddled elderly residents. She could not recall one successful conclusion to a reputed theft. In the circumstances she decided to speak to the Matron first. When she arrived at the care home she was shown immediately into Matron's office, where she also found Dr Priest sipping a cup of black coffee.

"I've asked Dr Priest to help us, officer. He has treated Miss Stones for several years."

Dr Priest smiled at the policewoman. "What is she saying, then, officer?"

"I understand that Miss Stones claims she has had a valuable necklace taken from her room."

"When was this?" Dr Priest asked.

Matron answered this query: "She is not too sure, Doctor,

but she has accused a temporary member of staff."

Olive sought further information: "Is Miss Stones fully compos mentis, Doctor?"

"Well, she is like many patients with developing dementia – she has lucid periods followed by confused episodes. Her accusation might be genuine, of course. She was lucid when I examined her half an hour ago."

Matron made the obvious point: "So, officer, I suggest you speak to her right away."

"Could you accompany me, Matron? Your presence might help her remember accurately."

Dr Priest agreed with WPC Winsford's suggestion: "Good idea, officer. And I will stay here with my coffee, but call me if Miss Stones becomes aggressive."

In fact Ethel Stones was in one of her more aggressive moods. She was sitting by the window in her narrow room fuming inwardly. Matron knocked on her door and entered with the policewoman.

"Who are you and what do you want?"

"I am June Bailey, the Matron, and I have brought WPC Winsford here with me."

"Why?"

"If you think back to last night, Miss Stones, you will remember you told my staff that you have had a valuable necklace stolen. WPC Winsford needs to ask you some questions so she can clear the matter up for you."

Ethel Stones was not satisfied. She turned to WPC Winsford: "Well, young woman, you've taken your time getting here, but no matter. I know who stole my necklace and I want him arrested this instant."

Olive Winsford did her best to calm the elderly lady: "Good. Please tell me who you suspect and describe any evidence you have."

"I do not know the man's name, but he's a foreigner. He's come to our country; he's taken one of our jobs and my valuable necklace."

"And your evidence, Miss Stones?"

Olive's question inflamed Ethel Stones further: "Now look here, I'm telling you the foreigner did it – do you understand?"

Olive turned to the Matron: "Do you have a foreigner working here, Matron?"

"Yes, but only occasionally. He's called Dimitri Rotarescu."

"Can I speak to him now, Matron?"

"I'm afraid not, officer; he only works here on his days off from his other job at the local recycling centre."

Olive turned back to Miss Stones: "Please tell me how and when this man stole your necklace, Miss Stones."

"He came to my door in the night; I went to the toilet; he went into my room and he took my necklace."

"Did you see him enter your room?"

"It's obvious that he did."

"I'm afraid it isn't, Miss Stones. Now please describe the person you saw."

Ethel Stones controlled herself with great difficulty. "He was a short runt of a man – definitely a Gypsy. They'll steal anything, you know."

Olive turned to the Matron: "Do you recognise this person, Matron?"

"No, he is certainly not employed here."

Miss Stones erupted: "You damn people! You're all the same – totally incompetent. I'm going to complain to your superiors and write to the press."

Ethel Stones was even more incensed when neither woman reacted to her threats. Instead she heard Olive Winsford speak in a calm voice to June Bailey: "Matron, is there anybody who can help us here – another resident perhaps?"

"Unfortunately most of the people on this floor have limited mobility, officer, but there is Mr Weston from room 18 – he's fully mobile. I'll try and find him."

June Bailey was in luck because, as if by magic, Basil stepped out of the lift at the very moment when she went into the corridor.

"Ah, Mr Weston, I wonder if you can help us?"

"I'll do my best, Matron, but I must just visit the little boys' room first."

"I understand, Mr Weston. Now, when you've performed please come to my office – I won't keep you long."

As he urinated Basil tried to think of anything the police officer, whom he had spotted in room 15, might want to question him about – smoking in a public place was still lawful, surely! Before doing up his fly Basil had to wipe his right shoe – accurate urination was obviously not closely allied to deep thought. He flushed the toilet, washed his hands and tried to relax.

"Come in, Mr Weston." Matron's voice penetrated her office door.

Basil entered to find himself surrounded by three persons.

Matron took the lead: "Sit down next to Dr Priest, please, Mr Weston.

The Doctor smiled at Basil. "Good morning again, Mr Weston. Now, how's the smoking going?"

Basil made no reply to the Doctor's question; instead he looked over at the policewoman.

Matron continued to lead: "This is WPC Winsford, Mr Weston. She would like your help."

Basil expected the policewoman to intervene at this point; she didn't because Matron continued her leadership.

"Last night, Mr Weston – I'm not sure of the exact time – there was a disturbance on your floor concerning Miss Stones. She confronted a man she thought was a member of staff. Do you remember anything from the disturbance?"

"I remember her shouting and screaming last night, Matron, about something to do with a necklace; the nurse and that young foreigner tried to calm her down."

Olive Winsford took over the questioning: "Did you see or hear anything suspicious on any occasion previous to last night's events?"

Basil gave the question serious thought before answering: "Well, some nights ago I heard her talking to someone in the corridor. She wanted a glass of water, I believe, and that stimulated my bladder, so I got out of bed and went into the corridor. She wasn't there, but I caught sight of a bloke hurrying towards the backstairs."

WPC Winsford recognised that this information could be important.

"Did you recognise the foreign worker – I believe he's called Dimitri Rotarescu – Mr Weston."

"No. Now, let me be clear: I only saw a fleeting back view

and the bloke I saw was certainly too short and puny to be this Dimitri chap."

"Thank you, Mr Weston – you have been very helpful."

"May I go now, Matron?"

"Yes, Mr Weston."

As Basil stood up to leave, Dr Priest offered him a second intervention: "Right, Mr Weston, you've got time to smoke two more fags before lunch."

When Basil was safely out of the way Olive Winsford turned to the Matron: "Could some interloper enter the care home without being seen, do you think?"

June Bailey thought for a few seconds before she came up with a suggestion: "I'll call in one of my full-time male staff members – they cover the whole place on their various shifts."

Dr Priest had had enough: "I'd better be off, Matron. Call me if you have any problems with Miss Stones."

Sami Barroti was able to join the Matron and WPC Winsford in the office.

Matron jumped in to pose the first question: "Sami, have we ever had an interloper enter the home?"

"Not that I know of, Matron. The reception area is covered by CCTV and I check the footage each day."

Matron was satisfied, but Olive Winsford wasn't.

"Is there any other entrance?"

Sami paused for a second or two before he answered: "Well, there's the back door down by the laundry room, but it's kept locked; now, officer, I know it shouldn't be, in case there's a fire, but Matron and I decided to keep it locked for security reasons."

"But it could be opened to let someone in, I take it?"

Matron got her response in before Sami: "Yes, but none of the staff would dare break my rulings."

"But you employ temporary staff from time to time?"

Reluctantly Matron had to agree: "Yes, I do occasionally."

Sami's next remark uncovered a new dimension: "Matron, I've noticed a smell of tobacco in the laundry area on a couple of occasions."

"Surely not, Sami!"

"Yes, definitely. I haven't told you before because I was hoping to find out who is responsible."

Olive Winsford saw a fag end of opportunity. "Could it be this Dimitri Rotarescu?"

"It is possible, officer, because he does work in that area sometimes, but Matron sometimes employs a young woman."

Olive made sure her smartphone was recording Sami's answers.

"Do you know her name?"

"Yes, she's Stacie Holt, and judging by her accent I should say she is from the London area. She's become friendly with Mr Weston and they've both been seen smoking in town."

The policewoman was quick to thank Sami, but added, "Of course there's no real evidence that she was the smoker in the laundry or that she let someone else enter, but, Matron, I think it's a possibility you and your staff should be aware of. Is it possible for you to extend your CCTV system, for instance?"

"I hardly have enough funds available to maintain the present system, officer. Now, what can I tell Miss Stones when she next grills me?"

"I can't take the matter any further without more concrete, definite evidence, Matron, but, of course, you can say that the police have offered you advice and that you will be extra-vigilant."

June Bailey was about to protest, but WPC Winsford was saved by her smartphone, which began to ring.

"I must take this, Matron, and then I must leave. Please inform me if you have any further problems."

CHAPTER 16

Basil and Stacie had finished their afternoon smoking session and were now entering The Red Lion. Stacie went to sit by the window while Basil went to the bar to order two coffees. Syd Fawkes was behind the bar as usual.

"Afternoon, Basil. Two white coffees, is it? Oh, by the way, have you mentioned to your betrothed about the blokes who came in here looking for her and her boyfriend?"

Basil had to admit he hadn't: "No, Syd. See, we've had trouble at the home – the police have been called in."

"What's all that about, then?"

"Oh, it's probably a load of nonsense – there's this old bird who's partly off her rocker. She's says the foreign lad who works at the home sometimes has nicked her necklace."

"Have the cops arrested him, then, Basil?"

"There's no evidence, Syd. I've told them that I saw a bloke making a getaway some nights ago and it definitely wasn't the foreign lad."

"Your coffees will be getting cool, Basil; better take them to your lady friend or you could be for it."

Basil smiled. "Syd, I can't remember the last time I was for it with a lady."

"Nor me, Basil. But hey, remember to mention those two guys I told you about."

Basil put the coffees on a tray and carefully approached Stacie.

"What was all that about, Basil?"

"Oh, I was just telling Syd about some trouble at the care

home. Some old bird claims someone has stolen her necklace. The police questioned me earlier today."

Basil noticed Stacie tense up when she heard his information.

"Could you help the police at all, Basil?"

"No, not really. I saw someone a few nights ago moving quickly away from me down the first-floor corridor, but I couldn't identify him."

"So what happens now?"

"Nothing much is my guess. It's more than likely that the old bird has lost the necklace, if she even had it in her room in the first place. I've never seen her wear any jewellery."

Stacie relaxed and sipped her coffee.

Basil continued his narrative: "She's even accused that foreign chap – I can't remember his name right now?"

"Do you mean Dimitri?"

"Yes, that's him – nice chap, very accommodating."

Stacie said no more; her thoughts were also on the accommodating foreigner.

The couple stayed put for another few minutes before Stacie announced she had to leave. Basil took the coffee cups back to the bar.

"Did you mention anything about those two guys to your friend, Basil?"

"Oh, bollocks, I forgot, Syd! Never mind – I'll probably see her tomorrow."

Syd fancied that he was about to endure another clientless afternoon, but shortly after Basil had left the bar door opened and the two men who had asked questions the day before entered again. Both came to the bar.

"Well, hi again, gents. Now, what can I get you?"

The shorter individual, sporting the colourful tattoo, responded: "OK, we'll 'ave a couple of pints of best, but first tell us if you've seen the bloke we described to you yesterday."

Syd was aware he was on his own and that the newcomers seemed very aggressive again.

"No, I haven't actually seen him, but his partner was in here earlier – you missed her by about twenty minutes."

"Was she alone, then?" the taller man asked.

"No, she was with a friend. He's a resident at the local care home – she works there occasionally."

The tattooed specimen took up the questioning again: "Where is it, mate?"

"You can't miss it – it's in Church Walk at the end of the High Street, near the church."

"Come on, Billy, we'll go and find it."

"Shall I pour your beers now, gents?"

Neither man replied; both turned and left the bar. Syd considered that he was losing his touch.

Jed Wrench and Billy Albright had known Dave Pringle for a couple of years. All three could be said to be educational failures and, as such, finding permanent work was difficult for them. Sometimes they helped Jed's father clear out houses and flats when they became vacant; and it was through the connections they made that they became mules, delivering drugs mainly in South London. They branched out as they became more confident, and it was because of these better earning possibilities that Jed and Billy fell out with Dave. He had acquired some spice, but he lied to the others about the quantity; this allowed him to make a killing. Unfortunately for Dave, the other two found out about his scam. Jed had sent a threatening text and Dave, knowing Jed's violent nature, had decided to disappear for a period, taking Stacie with him. However, Dave's former colleagues did not write him off – they began to make enquiries, and it was from one of Stacie's friends, who knew she and Dave had come north to the West Midlands, that they gained a rough idea of where they were hiding out, somewhere in Staffordshire.

It took some time before Jed and Billy, through a process of elimination, alighted on the small market town of Chelford as their enemy's probable place of residence. Tracking down Stacie Holt was a major step forward. She wasn't their main target. However, she could lead them to their prey. But how? They sat on a bench in Church Terrace to discuss their next moves.

"Why don't we hang about by this care home, Jed? Pringle's bird will show up at some time, and when she's finished her shift we can follow her."

"Too much waiting around, Billy. No, we'll call in at the care home and say we're trying to contact my cousin Stacie."

"But she ain't your cousin, Jed."

"Of course she bloody isn't, but staff at the home won't know that, will they? I'll say we need to contact her urgently because of a family problem; I'll ask for her address up 'ere, see?"

Billy said nothing more – he had been out-thought again. Jed stood up and led the way towards the care home.

"Now, when we get in there let me do the talking."

Billy had no intention of disobeying his friend's order.

It was Val Davies' day off; Joan Setters was on duty at reception. Joan did not enjoy dealing directly with people or even answering the phone; she preferred active work. So she was on the back foot when two unknown young men approached her desk.

"Can I help you, gentlemen?"

Jed pushed in front of Billy.

"I'm looking for my cousin – I believe she works here."

"What is her name, please?"

"Holt – Stacie Holt. She's my cousin and I've got some important family news for her."

"She's not here at the moment, but I can check this evening's rota if you like."

Jed smiled at Joan. "Oh, yes, please."

The two men had to wait a few minutes before Joan was able to locate the appropriate page on her screen.

"Yes, she'll be in a little later today."

"Do you have her local address?"

Joan stared at Jed's tattoo before returning to her screen.

"I'm afraid not, but I have a landline number for her. Would you like it?"

Billy was amazed by Jed's response: "No, thanks, it will be better if I meet her face-to-face."

"I understand," Joan told him. "Now, you can wait in our lounge if you like."

"No, thanks, miss. We don't want to disturb anyone. Come on, Brian, we'll wait outside."

Once outside, Billy let rip his annoyance: "Why didn't you

get her number, Jed, and why did you call me Brian?"

"Because, thicko, Dave might have answered the phone. He would have recognised my voice and done a runner. The less these people know about us the better."

"But why couldn't we wait in the lounge, Jed?"

"I had a glance in the lounge when we first went in – there were near-corpses all over the bloody room. We'll find a hiding place somewhere in the grounds and we'll follow Dave's tart when she finishes her shift."

Once again Billy was trumped, but he was still determined to play a positive role.

"Look, Jed, down there at the back of the house there's some big rubbish bins; we could hide there and still have a view of the main entrance."

"Well spotted, Billy. I was just about to suggest the same thing."

In Dave's grandmother's bungalow Stacie was preparing herself for work.

"I'm off now, Dave; are you coming with me?"

Dave had spent another boring day, so a little thieving in the care home offered some excitement and possible riches.

"I'll be right with you, Stacie."

As they walked along, Stacie raised a sensitive subject: "Dave, someone at the home told me they'd smelled tobacco smoke in the laundry room."

"So?"

"Was it you?"

"Maybe."

"Well, look, they'll be checking and you don't want to be caught."

Dave didn't comment. He knew she was right, but he didn't want to admit it. They walked the rest of the way in silence.

Jed and Billy were not comfortable behind the rubbish bins. There was nowhere to sit and the smell was distinctly putrid. Jed was about to suggest he and Billy return to the pub when they both heard footsteps on the gravel drive. Jed peeped round the side of a bin before grabbing his friend's arm.

"It's him, Billy," he whispered fiercely.

"Who, Jed?"

"Pringle with his tart."

Billy tried to view their target, but was held back by Jed because Dave Pringle was coming directly towards the bins.

"Get your blade ready, Billy."

The rubbish bin was a large cylinder, so Jed was able to pull Billy to his left. Dave seemed to be heading to the right side of the bin. Jed wondered if he had been spotted, but he was reassured when Dave paused directly behind the bin.

Jed whispered fiercely in his friend's ear, "You go that way round the bin, Billy; I'll go the other way." Once they were in position Jed shouted out, "Get him now!"

Billy arrived a millisecond before Jed.

Dave turned to face Billy, who was waving a knife, but the voice he heard came from behind him: "Well, fancy meeting you here, twat head." Dave spun round and found himself face-to-face with a former friend, who continued his greeting: "We've had a right old time finding you, Dave, but here we are. We need our money and I do hope you've got it or Billy will have to use his blade. Show him your blade again, Billy."

Dave turned and came face-to-face with a kitchen knife.

"L-l-look," he stammered, "I've got your money."

"In your underpants, is it?" Jed asked.

"No, it's where I'm staying."

Jed wasn't convinced. "Really? How much, then?"

"I've got you a car?"

"Ferrari, is it?"

"No, Jed, it's a BMW."

"Now listen, you idiot – me and Billy are not joking here. You owe us and you haven't got a BMW, bugger you."

"I have, and if you come with me you can have it now."

"Keep your knife on him, Billy. Right, big boy, take us to this limousine – and you'd better not be messing us about."

Dave left his place behind the bin; Jed walked alongside him with Billy a step or two behind, holding the knife, which he had partly hidden up his sleeve. Dave walked quickly, thinking continuously.

Syd Fawkes was standing by the bar door as the threesome passed by on the other side of the street.

'So,' he thought, 'the non-customers have obviously made contact with their target.' Syd wondered whether Basil had spoken to Stacie.

Ten minutes later the threesome arrived at the bungalow.

"Where's this bloody car, then, Dave?"

"In the garage, Jed. I'll go and get the key for you."

"And we'll come with you. Cover 'im with your knife, Billy."

Dave led the other two into the kitchen and took the key from a drawer. He handed it to Jed.

"Here you are – the car's all yours."

"You're coming with us, Dave, while we have a look."

Once outside, Dave opened the garage door, and for a moment or two his former friends stood transfixed. The vehicle was certainly a BMW, and to Jed's surprise it was only about two years old.

"Billy, keep your eye and your knife on Dave while I back the car out."

Dave was relieved when the engine started first time while emitting several whiffs of smoke. Jed reversed out carefully then stopped the engine. He still had several questions.

"Right, Dave, how did you get hold of it?"

"A friend gave it to me."

"A friend who'd nicked it, then?"

It was no good denying it.

"Yes, but it's worth over 20,000 quid."

Jed made a quick examination of the exterior before his next question: "Got a form V5C for it, Dave?"

"What the hell is that?"

"They used to call it the logbook."

"No, I ain't got one, but, Jed, old Artie Shaw in Catford will know how to trade it on. I bet he'll give you 10,000 for it."

Jed knew this to be true, but he was still wary.

"Are the number plates genuine, Dave?"

"No, of course not – what do you take me for? Look, all you've got to do is drive it to London, contact Artie and collect the cash. It was nicked some time ago, so it won't be the main item on the Old Bill's radar."

144

Jed thought for a few seconds before agreeing: "OK, Dave, we'll call it quits. Get in the motor, Billy; we'll drive south when it's dark."

Dave felt intense relief as the car left his grandmother's driveway. It was now time to put more of his plan into action: he would ring the police and report a stolen vehicle."

Jed did not drive far.

He stopped in a lay-by on the edge of town and turned to Billy: "How do you fancy driving this beauty home, Billy? I'm happy to pick up our old camper van from the local campsite where we've been staying and I'll meet you later tonight at my place in Bermondsey."

Jed could see that Billy was very keen to drive the Beemer, so he opened the driver's door and left the vehicle.

"See you later, mate."

While Jed was making the transport arrangements Dave was on the phone from the bungalow. He didn't ring 999; instead he contacted the local police. Sergeant Locke took his call.

"You want to notify us of a suspicious vehicle, sir? Could you describe it, please?"

Dave gave a full description, including the false registration number.

"You say you think it was stolen from London some time ago, sir?"

Dave explained that he was up from London on holiday and before he had left he had heard a local radio report of the theft of a BMW of the same model and colour from the suburb of Barnes. Sergeant Locke then asked on which road he'd seen the car and whether Dave had had a good look at the driver. Dave said he hadn't because it was getting dark. The Sergeant thanked him and rang off. He was not sure the information was very helpful, but, because there was nothing else on this particular evening, he decided to make some checks, including from where in Chelford the call had been made.

Stacie was happy to find out that Dimitri would be with her in the kitchen. Maggie Reeder delegated them both to do the washing-up and then to clean all the surfaces.

Dimitri waited till Maggie had left before posing a question to his workmate: "Stacie, do you want some extra work?"

Stacie stopped emptying the dishwasher.

"Well, yes, if it's local and the pay is reasonable. What's the deal, Dimi?"

"I'm sure you've heard about the break-in at The Tip and how my two fellow workers were badly injured."

"Yes, I heard Sami telling Imran."

"Well, Jack Sugden, the boss at The Tip, wants to hire someone local to fill in. He's asked me as well."

"I know nothing about waste disposal, Dimi."

"I didn't either when I started, but there's nothing to it really: you just help people put their stuff in the right container, and if you're not sure which one either I or Mr Sugden would help."

The thought of working with Dimitri in a different environment was enough to conquer Stacie's doubts.

"OK, Dimi, I'll call in at the site tomorrow."

Maggie Reeder had left her underlings alone for once – much to the relief of Stacie and Dimitri, who had no idea where she had disappeared to. However, she returned, like a bad penny, just as they were finishing cleaning the kitchen. She looked rather flushed around the gills, and when she opened her mouth to speak a distinct smell of alcohol cancelled out the kitchen cleaning fluid. Maggie made a close inspection of the cleaned surfaces, then the floor. It was obvious that she was searching out areas where she could impose her will. At last she found something: "You have not emptied this waste bin; now bag it up and get rid of it."

This suited Stacie.

"I'll take it, Dimi; you can knock off and I'll see you tomorrow at The Tip."

She picked up the plastic sack and made her way to the rear entrance. She now had an ideal excuse to unlock the back door, but to her surprise when she tried to open the door it remained locked. Suddenly, someone emerged from the laundry – it was Sami.

"Can you open the door for me, Sami? Ms Reeder wants me to get rid of this rubbish."

Sami smiled at her. "I'm sorry about this, Stacie, but it appears someone may have been entering the home at night. Matron has asked me to keep a close eye on the situation. You see, someone has definitely been smoking in the laundry. You like a cigarette, don't you?"

"Yes, Sami, but not while I'm at work – and anyway these days I help out in the kitchen. Ms Reeder would stick my head in the microwave if she caught me smoking."

Sami laughed out loud. "OK, Stacie. Now look, we've had this new lock fitted; it has a code number. I'll tap it in for you."

The door swung open.

"There you are."

"Could you tell me the number, please, Sami? If not I'll have to find you each time I need to bring the rubbish, and I don't think Ms Reeder will be too pleased either."

The cook's name did the trick.

"Right, Stacie, I'll give it to you. It's dead simple – 4321. Even I can remember it."

Sami smiled again and left Stacie to her task. Once outside, Stacie tried to find Dave, without success. She was worried, so, as her shift was almost ended, she decided to hurry to the bungalow.

After making the phone call to the police Dave was feeling very relaxed. He decided to treat himself to a drink in The Red Lion. For once there were several customers in the bar watching the large television screen, on which Dave's favourite team, Crystal Palace, were labouring against the might of Arsenal.

"Good evening, sir. Now, what can I get you?"

Dave turned away from the screen and faced Syd Fawkes. "I'll have a pint of bitter."

"You're not with your partner tonight, then?"

"No, she's at work."

Syd smiled. "That's what I like to hear – a bloke watching the soccer while his other half earns the money. Incidentally, there are a couple of blokes looking for you; they've been in here twice without buying a drink. Have they found you yet?"

Dave realised he had to say something. "Yes, I've seen them and everything is sorted, thanks."

"One of them had the best tattoo I've ever seen."

"Oh yeah, that's my mate, Jed. Now I'd better watch the game – Palace need my support."

Syd realised that the small talk was over,

Stacie had a big shock when she arrived back at the bungalow:the garage was open and the car had vanished. Had Dave upped and left? She hurried into the bungalow to find out. There was no sign of her lover, but his clothes were still in the wardrobe. Stacie wondered if he was just giving the car a run. She decided to try his mobile, but while she was dialling she heard a car on the drive. She put the handset down and hurried outside, where she had a second even bigger shock: a police car and two officers confronted her.

Stacie attempted to take the initiative: "Can I help you, officer?"

WPC Olive Winsford answered her: "I'm here with my colleague, PC Spanier, to speak to someone who called the local station earlier this evening. Was it you by any chance?"

"No, I've been at work – you can check with the local care home."

"Can we go indoors, please?"

Stacie was becoming more anxious by the second. She said nothing, but turned and walked back into the bungalow; both police officers followed her. Once inside, Stacie noticed that both officers were casting their eyes everywhere.

"My sergeant took the call; he told me it was a male voice." Olive Winsford stared at Stacie as she said this.

Stacie sought to play for time: "It might have been my partner, officer. He's not in trouble, is he?"

"No, no, just the opposite. His information has meant a person driving a stolen car has been arrested. It's probably a good job he didn't confront this person himself because the thief was armed."

Stacie sat down on a kitchen chair with a traffic jam of thoughts crushed into her mind.

The officer carried on: "What is your partner's name, may I ask? My sergeant needs it for his report, you see."

"Oh, he's Dave."

"Dave who?"

This presented Stacie with a huge problem because Dave had a criminal record.

She decided to lie: "Dave Prentice."

"Thank you. Now, when your partner gets back here please ask him to contact Sergeant Locke at the local police station; the Sergeant needs a few more details before the thief goes to court on trial."

Dave Pringle, now Prentice, was on his way back home from the pub. He was not in a good mood because he had just watched Arsenal thrash Crystal Palace; his mood worsened as he arrived at the bungalow and saw the police car parked on the drive. He walked on past the open gate, crossed the road and hid behind a low privet hedge. He did not have to wait long before the police car reversed out, turned and drove off into the gloom. Dave didn't hang about – he raced back across the road and entered the relative safety of the bungalow, where he found Stacie sitting by the kitchen table.

"What the balls is going on, Stacie?"

"The police have been here."

"I know the bloody police have been here. What did they want?"

To Dave's surprise Stacie smiled at him. "You're a hero, Dave."

"What the—?" He got no further.

"They told me you rung up about a stolen car."

"How the hell did they find that out? You didn't tell them, did you?"

"No, of course I didn't! They obviously traced your call. You should have used your pay-as-you-go mobile. Anyway, they told me they've arrested the driver and recovered the vehicle."

"Did they say who the driver was?"

"No, Dave, they didn't, but they did say he was armed."

"How many did they arrest?"

"They mentioned just the one."

"Oh, shit!"

"Why the poo, Dave?"

Dave didn't answer the question; instead he posed one of his own: "Did you give them my name, Stacie?"

"No, of course not – I'm not stupid."

Dave relaxed a little. "So what did they want?"

"They want you to contact the Sergeant so you can give him more details. And now, Dave, I have a question: "Where is the BMW?"

Dave offered no explanation; he sat down opposite Stacie and he was clearly deep in thought.

Stacie spent a restless night because Dave came late to bed. He was obviously having problems sleeping because he got up three times and he was clearly distracted by something or somebody. He finally fell into a fitful sleep at four in the morning.

Stacie got up at seven; she had a shower and made herself breakfast. She left a note for Dave, informing him that she had gone to The Tip to seek extra work.

CHAPTER 17

Jack Sugden was not a happy supervisor because he was faced with another day with too few staff. He was surprised, however, when he arrived at The Tip because two people were waiting for him. He recognised Dimitri straight away, but not the young waif of a lass who was with him.

"Good morning, sir. This is Stacie Holt. She'd like a job if possible."

Jack looked the young woman up and down. From her appearance and physique he doubted whether she could lift a bag of crisps never mind a sack of rubbish, but needs must when there was a staff shortage.

Jack smiled at the female. "Good morning, Stacie. Now, when my administrator arrives I'll ask her to interview you, so please follow me to the office."

Stacie smiled at Dimitri and followed Jack to the Portakabin.

Mollie Knowles arrived five minutes later and Jack put her in the picture before turning to Stacie: "I've got to open up now, Miss Holt, so I'll leave you in the tender care of Mrs Knowles here."

Mollie realised that, once again, she'd been passed a buck, although in this instance it was more like a frail doe.

"Please have a seat, Stacie. Now, have you ever worked in a recycling facility before?"

"No." Clearly here was a young woman of definite brevity.

"How did you find out about the job?"

"Dimi – I mean, Dimitri – told me about it.

"Has he told you what we do here?"

"Yes."

"And do you think you can cope if appointed?"

"Yes. He said he can help me."

"How do you know Dimitri, may I ask?"

"Sometimes we work together at the Town End Care Home."

This was good news for Mollie because she could contact the care home and speak to her friend Val Davies, so she smiled at Stacie.

"What I can do, Stacie, is to offer you a trial period of, say, a fortnight, to see if you like the job and if you can cope with the workload. Now, how does that sound?"

"Fine. I can start now if you like."

"All right, tell Mr Sugden – he's by the residual-waste container – and then help your friend Dimitri."

Once Stacie had left the office, Mollie phoned her old school friend Val Davies at the care home.

"Is that you, Val?"

"Yes. Now, who am I speaking to, please?"

"It's Mollie here – you know Pretty Knowles from the sixth form."

"How are you, Moll?"

"Fine, I suppose, but I'm not sure how long my job will last; how about you?"

"In the same state, Moll – my job could go at any moment. Now, how can I help?"

"I've just signed on a temporary worker; her name is Stacie Holt and she tells me she's done some work at the care home, so I'm just ringing to ask whether she's reliable and can she be trusted?"

"Well, Mollie, she's always turned up for work on time and she does a reasonable job. I mean, not many can put up with working for Maggie Reeder. But on the trust front you need to be careful – her partner is a surly young lout, so I've heard – but she's probably worth a try. Incidentally, how are your two workers who were injured in that robbery?"

"Well, Val, Fred Urmston is making a good recovery, but Pete Fenton is still in an induced coma. Anyway, I must ring off – I think the big boss has just arrived. Thanks for the info."

George Rampling was on-site, but he did not come directly to the office; instead he went to talk to Jack Sugden.

"Morning, Jack. I've just come to see how things are going without the injured men. I see that foreign bloke is still here, but who's the young woman?"

"She's Stacie Holt, Mr Rampling. Mrs Knowles has just hired her because, as you know, we're very short of staff."

"She's on a temporary contract, I take it."

"Oh, I'm sure she is, sir."

"Good, because there's an important council meeting this evening when the Finance Department will present their proposals for savings in the next financial year."

"Do you know any details, Mr Rampling?"

"Not at the moment, Jack, but I know that Tobias Argent has been poking his prejudices in. Right, I'll just go and have word with Mrs Knowles – I'll tell her exactly what I've told you."

Dave Pringle was still in a wary state of mind; he was pretty certain that the police had arrested Billy Albright, but he was unsure about the whereabouts of Jed Wrench, who he knew would be furious if the BMW was in police hands.

"Would Jed be able to work out why the police had acted so quickly after he and Billy had taken possession of the car? Dave knew that Jed was intelligent, so he had probably let Billy drive the car alone because of the risks involved. Dave also knew that his plan to take the car to Glasgow was now impossible. He needed extra cash soon, so he must continue stealing from the care home, but he really did need something valuable to go with the necklace and the medals. His chain of thought was interrupted by the phone. Dave answered it, but attempted a Scottish accent in case Jed was on the line.

Actually his caller was Val Davies from the care home: "Could I speak to Miss Holt, please?

"I'm afraid she's not here, but I can give her a message."

"Right, tell her we have work for her this evening from seven till midnight and ask her to confirm whether she is available."

"She is definitely available; I'm her partner and I'll make sure she's there on time."

Dave decided to visit his partner at The Tip immediately so

she could definitely make an appearance in the care home. He walked for ten minutes or so before arriving at his destination. Everything seemed very relaxed – there were no vehicles unloading and for a minute or two Dave could not spot where Stacie was. He entered the compound and spotted her; she was chatting to a tall bloke behind the small-appliances container.

"Stacie! Stacie! I need a word with you."

Stacie dropped her lighted cigarette to the floor and said something to the tall bloke before she approached Dave.

"What are you doing here, Dave?"

"Who's that bloke you're chatting up, Stacie?"

"Oh, he's just someone who works here – he's my trainer, actually. Anyway, why are you here?"

"You've had a call from the care home – they want you to do a shift this evening from seven till midnight; I've told them you'll do it."

Stacie looked hard at her lover. "Well, thank you, Dave."

Dave attempted to moderate his attitude; he took Stacie by the elbow and dropped his voice: "Look, Stacie, it gives me a great opportunity to nick a few more things."

"You'll have to be very careful, Dave, because the deputy – he's called Sami – is carrying out regular checks on the laundry area after he smelled your cigarette smoke."

Stacie had made her point and she didn't have to point out that Dave had brought the problem on himself; instead she gave him some more information: "They've changed the lock on the back door, Dave, and it's got a code number, 4321, so if you can remember it you can let yourself in; you don't need me to open up for you. Now look, there are a couple of cars entering the compound so I've got to get back to work. I'll see you sometime."

Dave walked back to the bungalow feeling rather confused. He usually called the shots, but today Stacie was the most assertive he could ever remember; on the other hand, he now had much easier access to the residents' rooms.

Jed Wrench was very angry. He had returned to his flat in Bermondsey expecting to find Billy Albright and the BMW. At first he wasn't too bothered, but as the hours passed he became more and more agitated. Would Billy have had the initiative and nous to trade the car on himself without involving him? He thought this highly unlikely. Perhaps the police had stopped Billy en route – after all, the car had been stolen. Although the theft had been carried out weeks ago and the number plates were false, the police would still have it on their radar. The more Jed thought about it the more he suspected that Dave Pringle had tipped off the Old Bill. It was quite clear that the money Pringle owed would now remain unpaid unless, of course, Jed returned to Staffordshire and forced Pringle to cough up. Jed knew that Dave was totally untrustworthy, so to get to the facts he would need a weapon to frighten him. He decided against taking a knife because he would have to get close to Dave to scare him and he recognised that Dave was bigger and stronger than he was. He was lying in bed half asleep when he had a brainwave: a blowtorch! He had one in the kitchen cupboard which he had used some years ago in a burglary. Yes, he would take the blowtorch, and he would corner Dave with the torch lit. That would make the bastard reveal where he had some loot stashed.

Dave did not go to the care home with Stacie on this particular evening; he waited in the bungalow till late. He needed money, especially now with the BMW unavailable. His plan to go to Glasgow, where his great aunt lived, was off the programme; his only option was to return to London, but that brought dangers. Jed Wrench was not the only person in London who was a threat, but at least in London there would be more opportunities to earn.

Dave left the bungalow at eleven and walked through the quiet streets to the care home. He did not need Stacie to help him enter any more, but he decided to use his proven method of hiding behind the rubbish bins for a short time to make sure everything was quiet.

He went towards his usual vantage point, but suddenly out of the gloom he heard a familiar voice: "Why, good evening, Mr Pringle – great to meet you again."

Dave recognised the voice despite the upmarket phraseology: Jed Wrench! Dave turned to run, but Jed was after him and

Dave felt something hot close to his face.

"Come 'ere, you little bastard!"

Dave had no intention of coming anywhere near Jed. He ran towards the care home's main gateway, but Jed moved to cut him off. Dave turned and sprinted towards the care home's rear door; Jed skidded to a halt on the gravel drive and fell. This gave Dave a chance to reach the back door and enter the code, 4321. His intention now was to slam the external door shut, but Jed was too close so he turned into the laundry room, slammed that door shut and pulled the bolt into the locked position. Jed was now in the corridor and he knew where Dave was hiding.

"I'm going to burn you out of there!" he yelled. As he said this he trained his blowtorch on the door frame.

Inside the laundry Dave fished out his mobile phone and tried to dial the police – unfortunately he was out of battery. He could see smoke seeping through the door frame, so he started to yell for help. Jed concentrated on directing the torch flame and missed the fact that the external door had closed behind him.

Sami had been expecting a quiet night at the reception desk. He was snoozing in Val Davies' chair when a burning smell assaulted his nostrils. He knew immediately that it wasn't cigarette smoke, so he reached for the phone to report a suspected appliance fire. Suddenly the ceiling sprinklers burst into action and a body came running towards him. Sami stood and attempted to block the fugitive's passage. Whoever it was shoved Sami aside, dropping something hot as he did so. Dimitri appeared from the lounge and tripped the runner, who fell heavily, swearing. Dimitri sat on him while Sami sprayed the still burning blowtorch with a fire extinguisher. Other persons were now piling into the reception area – the local fire brigade had arrived together with two policemen. There was mayhem for several minutes; many of the residents were screaming. Ethel Stones demanded to know what the hell was going on.

At last some semblance of normality was restored. The police arrested Jed. Two firemen put out the fire in the laundry area and found a soggy, coughing Dave, whom they handed over to the police. Stacie helped calm the residents, as did

Dimitri when the police had relieved him of Jed Wrench. No one had much sleep, however, because the firemen stayed in situ for the rest of the night.

"So, Matron, please tell me what happened last night." Dr Priest posed the question the next morning as he sat in June Bailey's office without his usual black coffee.

June was not looking her normal immaculate self – she had been wakened in the night by Sami and had been at the home since 2 a.m.

"I'm not absolutely sure, Doctor, but the police should be here any minute to give me as many facts as they can. It seems that there was a dispute between two young men – neither was local, of course – and one tried to set fire to the other using a blowtorch. The intended victim got into the laundry somehow and locked himself in, and the aggressor tried to burn the door down; this set off the sprinkler system in that part of the building." June Bailey was forced to stop because Val Davies entered the office without knocking.

"Matron, Sergeant Locke is here."

The Sergeant had also had a broken night. He came into the office and sat next to Dr Priest.

"Right, Matron, I can tell you this: both men involved have been arrested on several charges, vehicle theft, drug dealing, attempted murder and arson amongst them. One of their former accomplices, arrested in London for car theft, has come clean, so they both will be sent down. There is one thing we can't quite work out, however." The Sergeant paused. "Could I have a cup of coffee by any chance, Matron?"

"Could you make that two, please?" The Doctor also needed a pick-me-up.

"Yes, yes, I'll just go and ask Mrs Davies."

Matron left the room.

Dr Priest turned to the policeman: "This is a bad business, Sergeant."

"It certainly is, but it could have been worse but for two immigrants who work here: one from Indonesia raised the alarm and another, from Romania, restrained one of the men till we arrived."

157

Matron re-entered her office.

"Mrs Davies is arranging the coffees, gentlemen. Now, Sergeant, you mentioned that something was puzzling you."

"Yes, that's right. You see, you have a secure rear door with a code number, so how did the two criminals enter that way? They didn't enter through the front entrance because CCTV would have filmed them."

Matron was also puzzled.

"Who knows the code number, Matron?"

"Well, I do and so do a few members of staff, but I hope you are not going to accuse any of them, Sergeant."

"No, I'm not right now, but the interloper, named Dave Pringle, obviously entered first so he must have learned it from someone."

"We need to speak to Sami Barroti, Sergeant – he's in charge of security." Matron was about to leave her office again, but Val Davies arrived with the coffees. "Ask Sami to join us, please, Mrs Davies."

"Certainly, Matron. He's in reception."

Within seconds Sami, looking very worried, entered the office and stood with his hands together in front of his groin.

Matron took the lead: "You have nothing to worry about, Sami, but the Sergeant here needs to find out who on the staff knows the code number for our rear entrance."

Sami continued to look stressed. "Well, I do and so does Imran – he deputises for me sometimes – and, oh, young Stacie because she takes out the rubbish."

"And is that everyone, Sami?"

"Yes, Matron – apart from yourself, of course."

Dr Priest stifled a giggle.

Sergeant Locke now took the initiative: "Thank you, Sami, and well done last night."

"Thank you, sir. May I leave now?"

"I have no further questions, Sami. Do you, Matron?"

"No, no. Sami, you may return to your duties."

When he had left, Sergeant Locke attempted to take the investigation further: "I need to speak to this Stacie, Matron."

"She's not here, Sergeant, but I believe she has another job at the local recycling centre. Perhaps you should try there."

"Thank you, Matron. I'll leave you now, but I promise to keep you informed of any developments."

When the Sergeant had left, Matron shared her worries with the Doctor: "This will be the end of the home, Doctor."

"Why do you say that, Matron?"

"The local council has to make massive savings; the damage caused here last night adds to their overheads. The laundry is out of service, which means I must pay for some other provider; in addition there are essential repairs needed as well. I'm talking thousands of pounds."

Doctor Priest understood her worries and decided to do what he could to support the home.

"Matron, the last thing many of your elderly, infirm residents need is extra stress. There are several who cannot possibly cope with an enforced move – they will probably die." The Doctor paused before adding, "Mind you, I suppose a few deaths will lower the council's expenses. Now listen: if the powers that be try to close you down, please let me know and I'll make the strongest case I can for the home to stay open from a medical point of view."

"Thank you, Doctor."

Dr Priest adopted a pained expression before his next remarks: "Our nation is showing less and less compassion for the needy, Matron. We are now a nation of many losers and a few winners, and if Winston Churchill was still alive I have no doubt he would sum up the situation in these words: 'Never before in the history of economic conflict has so much been taken from so many by so few.'"

June Bailey smiled despite her worries. "We must seek the glowing uplands again, Doctor, so today could you please start by examining Ethel Stones?"

"Yes, of course, and perhaps we ought to let Miss Stones confront the powers that be when the time for closure comes."

Over at The Tip Mollie Knowles was surprised when a police car pulled up in the designated parking area; she was even more surprised when a police sergeant came straight to the office without approaching the supervisor. Mollie opened the door to greet the officer.

"Good morning, Sergeant. I hope none of us here is in any trouble."

"Probably not, madam, but I need to speak to a Stacie Holt. Is she here by any chance?"

"Yes, she's over by the small-appliances container; shall I get her for you?"

"Please, and could I use your office for a few minutes? My conversation with Miss Holt should not be long."

"Of course you can, Sergeant. Oh, by the way, is there any news of our ex-employee Winston Green?"

"Two police forces are still trying to find him; they've had no luck so far. He may try to return to this town, of course, so please keep your eyes peeled."

"What does he need me for, Mrs Knowles?"

Mollie was now with Stacie by the small-electrical-items container.

"He didn't say exactly, but I shouldn't worry because he's promised I can have my office back in a few minutes. I'll keep my eye on this container while you speak to him."

Stacie hurried to the office hoping to get things over quickly.

"You are Miss Holt, I take it."

"Yes."

"And you know your friend David Pringle was arrested last night?"

"Yes, well, I guessed as much because he didn't return to the bungalow where we are staying."

"Please don't worry, Miss Holt – there is no suspicion attached to you – but you may be able to help me with my investigation; you see, it's obvious that your friend knew the code number for the care home's rear entrance; did you give it to him? I know you were told it so you could carry out your duties."

Stacie felt stumped and made no immediate attempt to answer the question.

Sergeant Locke sought to encourage her: "Look, Stacie, we know all about David Pringle's activities and the fact you were not directly involved, so I repeat my question; did you give him the code number?"

"Yes, I told him about the new method of entering the home just in passing, like."

"Thank you, Stacie. Now your friend will be brought to court and I'll try to keep you from being called as a prosecution witness. What is your present address, please?"

"I'm staying in a bungalow in Brookhouse Close."

"It belongs to David Pringle's grandmother, I believe."

"Yes, but I won't be there long – his grandma's due back from Spain soon."

"Where will you live then?"

Stacie shrugged her shoulders. "Dunno."

"You must let me know when you do leave – do you understand?"

"Yes. Can I go back to work now?"

"Yes, but remember what I have told you."

Stacie said no more. She turned and left the office. Mollie saw her leave and hurried back to the office.

"Is everything OK, Sergeant?"

"Yes – I think I may have just inserted the last piece of the jigsaw."

"Really, Sergeant, you do surprise me."

As the Sergeant drove off Mollie's mobile rang.

"Hi, Mollie. It's me – Nora. I've just seen a cop leave your place. Is everything OK?"

"Yes, thanks, Nora. No one is for the electric chair – the Sergeant just wanted some information from our latest recruit. I did ask him about Winston Green, who used to work here before he did a runner after the first robbery, but it seems the young man has disappeared."

"So, there are no additional problems, then?"

"No, not for the moment, Nora – let's hope it lasts."

161

CHAPTER 18

Stacie was aware that she had not told the Sergeant the whole story about her actions at the care home. There was the necklace Dave had stolen from Miss Stones, and Stacie was worried that the police might come with a warrant to search the bungalow. She decided to do her own search before any police action; she knew where Dave had stashed the necklace, but had he stolen anything else? She started her investigation in the main bedroom. She soon found the necklace, but that was all. The second bedroom was almost bare apart from a single bed and an empty chest of drawers. She tried the bathroom next and remembered that Dave had once told her he had hidden some drugs in an airing cupboard. It seemed that the necklace was Dave's only theft, but when she emptied a drawer in the kitchen she had a major find: she pulled out three medals. She was puzzled at first, but when she turned one over there was a name etched into the back which read, 'DVR E. J. Weston RFA'. She examined the other two very closely: unlike the first, which was star-shaped, the other two were circular and the same name was etched into both rims. Stacie knew at once where Dave had purloined them: from Basil's bedroom. She now had a quandary: should she auction off the items or return them to their rightful owners?

She did not like Ethel Stones but, on the other hand, Basil Weston had been a real friend and he was the only male in her life who had not sought to exploit her in some way or other. She decided to return the items secretly when she next worked at the care home.

It was Wednesday – a day when The Tip was closed. Stacie was pleased that the care home had offered her an extra daytime shift cleaning residents' bedrooms; she had agreed to work an evening shift as well. This schedule offered her the opportunity to replace the items stolen by her ex-lover. Residents who were fit enough rested in the lounge while their rooms were cleaned. Stacie made sure she knew who was in the lounge before starting her cleaning routine. She saw Ethel Stones sitting by the main window – she appeared to be asleep. However, there was no sign of Basil. Stacie went to find Joan Setters, who arranged the cleaning schedule.

"Good morning, Mrs Setters. Do you want me to clean room 18 today, please?"

Joan scrutinised her list before answering Stacie: "No, not this morning, Miss Holt. I understand that Mr Weston has had a disturbed night, so he requires extra sleep. Please be very quiet in the area of his room. Now, I suggest you start with room 15 because Miss Stones is resting in the lounge."

Stacie was very pleased because it gave her an ideal opportunity to replace the stolen necklace, which she now had in her apron pocket. She gathered her materials and equipment before taking the lift to the first floor.

Everything was quiet in the corridor so Stacie entered room 15 confidently. Once inside, she considered where best to leave the necklace; Dave had told her from where he had taken the item. Stacie did not replace it in the chest of drawers because it had been searched when Ethel Stones had first reported the necklace missing. Stacie thought for a few moments before deciding to hide it under the mattress; she had to change the bed sheets, so it seemed the obvious place.

She was in the process of lifting one end of the mattress when the door opened and a familiar voice assaulted her eardrums: "And what do you think you are doing, young lady?"

Stacie turned to face her interrogator with the necklace still in her hand.

She needed to improvise: "I've found your necklace, Miss Stones – it was under your mattress."

"Nonsense, girl! That is not my necklace; that is a piece of cheap tat. You are welcome to it."

Stacie was about to put the necklace back in her apron, but

was interrupted again, this time by Sami, who had heard raised voices from out in the corridor.

"I must ask what is going on here, ladies?"

Ethel Stones responded first: "This young woman is under the impression she has found my missing necklace."

Stacie managed to insert an explanation: "I found it under the mattress as I was about to change the sheets, Sami."

Ethel Stones would still have none of it: "It is definitely not my necklace; it is a mere trinket, as you can see. The young woman can keep it because I wouldn't be seen dead wearing it."

Sami looked at Stacie. "Follow me, Miss Holt, please, and bring the necklace."

Stacie complied with Sami's order.

Once in the corridor he spoke again, this time in a low voice: "I'll take the necklace, Stacie – it's definitely hers. I'll put it in the safe, then wait a few days before showing it to her again. My guess is she will then accept it as being hers. Well done for finding it." He smiled at Stacie, who returned to her cleaning duties.

Stacie was not allowed to enter room 18 because Dr Priest had insisted that Basil Weston must rest. The rest of her shift consisted of the usual back-aching work she was becoming accustomed to. When the shift finished Stacie went to The Red Lion for lunch because her earning power had increased and she was wary of returning to the bungalow. When she entered the pub she had a shock because there, sitting in his usual place, was the wide-awake Basil drinking a pint of beer. Stacie hurried over to him.

"I thought you were ill, Basil."

He looked up at her while wiping froth from his upper lip.

"I'm just having a restorative drinky and in a minute I'm going for a smokey; would you care to join me?"

"Yes, all right, but are you sure you'll be OK?"

"We must remember, Stacie, that doctors have to play safe. OK, I didn't sleep too well, but I'm not dead yet! Now, what will you have?"

Stacie spent the rest of the afternoon in a maze of burgers, fags and booze. She left Basil at five to prepare herself for the evening shift. She realised she could have returned the medals personally to Basil during their orgy, but she was worried he would be annoyed and ditch her so she reverted to her previous plan to return them when he was either out of his room or asleep.

As usual, in the evening Stacie had to work in the kitchen with the temperamental Maggie Reeder. Fortunately Dimitri was also on duty so she had someone to chat to.

"Are you planning to return to your country or will you stay in Britain permanently, Dimi?"

"I will probably return sometime soon, Stacie, when I have saved enough."

"But you could stay here?" Stacie asked this in hope.

"Possibly, Stacie."

Any further conversation was ended when Maggie Reeder called out to them, "Cut the cackle and clean those damn surfaces, you two."

An hour later Stacie excused herself from the kitchen, claiming falsely that she needed to visit the toilet. Instead she went up to room 18 and listened at the door. From inside she heard regular, deep breathing. She opened the door carefully and entered. The breathing continued, so Stacey crept to the window sill, where in the dim light she found the brass box. She took out the medals from her apron pocket and put them beside the box, which she then attempted to open. She was shocked when she heard some metallic sounds from inside. She froze, motionless. Fortunately Basil's regular breathing continued unabated. Stacie opened the box and, as quietly as she could, inserted the stolen medals. She closed the lid and then deliberately and very carefully she replaced it on the window sill. She took a deep breath and turned, intending to leave the room. She glanced towards the bed. Basil's head was propped up on his pillow; his eyes were open and staring straight at her. Stacie froze in panic. Basil's stare continued for a few seconds before his eyes closed and his breathing became deep and regular again.

Stacie dashed from the room trembling. Everything was calm in the corridor, so she rushed back to the kitchen.

"Well, you've taken your time! Total constipation, was it?"

Stacie had no chance to reply because Dimitri made his

presence felt: "Really, Ms Reeder, leave her alone. Younger women than you have monthly needs – perhaps you remember them."

His put-down worked: Maggie left the kitchen in a huff.

Later, when she had returned to the bungalow, Stacie began seriously to consider her situation without Dave. She knew she could only stay in the bungalow till Dave's grandmother returned; she had no idea when this would happen, and as she had never met Dave's relative she could not be sure that she would be allowed to stay. Should she return to London? The problem here was that, although she had a key to Dave's flat, she had no desire to live there until Dave got out of gaol. She fell asleep with her problems unresolved.

The next day Stacie was hired for just the morning shift. As she arrived she noticed the Doctor parking his car. He was accompanied by a nurse, so clearly someone needed extra attention. As Stacie entered the reception area she saw a large notice propped up on the desk; it announced that everyone should attend a short staff meeting at ten o'clock in Matron's office.

"Do I have to attend, please?" Stacie asked Val Davies.

"Yes, Miss Holt. As the notice says, the meeting is for everyone except Sami and the practice nurse who has just arrived with Dr Priest."

It was a very tight squeeze in Matron's office when everyone had convened. Stacie found herself standing behind Dimitri, so she could hardly see Matron when June Bailey stood up to speak.

"I have had to call this meeting this morning following a phone call I received earlier today."

She was interrupted by a loud familiar voice: "Matron, Sami is not here!"

June responded immediately: "He is not here, Ms Reeder, because someone has to keep their eye on our residents; Dr Priest has kindly brought his practice nurse to care for residents who are bed-bound. Now, as I was about to say, last evening our local councillors made a decision which affects us all. This care home will close within a few months."

The audience received the news in shocked silence before

Maggie Reeder spoke up again: "What will happen to our jobs, Matron?"

"I can give you no clear answer on that at the moment. Residents who are paid for by the local authority will have to be found places in other care homes; those who pay for themselves – like Basil Weston, for instance – will have to find placements on their own initiative. I'm sure some of you will be offered further employment, but obviously not in Chelford."

The audience's mood darkened and several voices called out, overwhelming June Bailey's attempted comments.

At last Dr Priest thumped Matron's desktop and shouted out, "Now, listen to me, all of you! None of this is Matron's fault – she is merely the messenger. If you want to protest I strongly suggest you approach your local councillor and our local Member of Parliament!"

June Bailey recovered her composure. "You must all now return to your duties; as always, our residents come first."

The staff turned and made for the door with many muttering their displeasure. When they had all gone June slumped into her chair.

"Thank you for your support, Doctor."

"This is yet another case of political policy being put before compassion, Matron. Several of the residents will not survive the enforced change, and staff must now seek other work so we will be in for turmoil. I'm particularly worried about residents like Basil Weston; he's totally alone in the world. If you don't mind, I'll inform him now of the council's decision and try to help him find a solution."

"Please do, Doctor, and let me know how he reacts."

Dr Priest found Basil in his room sitting by the window.

"Good morning, Mr Weston. I'm glad I've caught you here."

"I'm not sleeping too well, Doctor, but I am trying to cut down on the ciggies."

"Excellent, Mr Weston! Now I'll just take your blood pressure – hopefully it will have descended from the stratosphere." The Doctor made no further comments while taking the reading. "Well, it's down a little, Mr Weston, so you are being very sensible."

To his surprise Basil asked a relevant question, which helped broach the subject the Doctor wanted to discuss: "What was the meeting about, Doctor?"

"I'm glad you asked me that, Mr Weston, and I'm afraid I have some disquieting news."

"You're going to tell me the care home has to close, aren't you, Doctor?"

"Well, yes, but how did you find out?"

"I read the local newspaper and I follow the local news on the radio and television; it's been clear to me for some time that this place is under threat of closure."

"What will you do?"

"Well, I'd be grateful if you can listen to an idea I've had."

"Fire away, please."

"I have enough money in the bank to buy a small place in this town – something terraced with a couple of bedrooms."

"But could you manage on your own?"

"Not without help, no."

"I'm sorry to tell you this, Mr Weston, but carers do not come cheap."

"I know that, Doctor, so my idea is this: I'm friendly with a young lass who works here from time to time; she's highly vulnerable and on her own. Now, when I have my own home, I can offer her a bed and board if she will do some cleaning, shopping and cooking for me. What do you think?"

"People will talk, Mr Weston – I can hear them now: 'Dirty old devil having it off with that young slut.'"

"I'm sure you're right, Doctor, but I can admit here and now that I haven't had an erection since the last Labour government was in power. I could put a notice to that effect in the front window."

Dr Priest laughed, but then became serious: "You know the young woman is vulnerable, and I have to say this: your life expectancy is limited. So what will happen when you hit the heavens?"

"I've thought of that too, Doctor. I have no living relatives and all my friends are comfortably off, so I'll make a will leaving my assets, including the property, to her."

"And you'd tell her that, would you?"

"Yes, definitely."

"So you can really trust her, can you?"

"Yes, and I have some evidence. Last night she sneaked into my room and replaced my father's First World War medals; I watched her do it."

"She might have stolen them in the first place, you know."

"That is possible, Doctor, but it is much more likely that her horrible boyfriend did it. He, incidentally, has been arrested on serious charges, according to the local media."

"Well, I hope you are right, Mr Weston, and I admire you for giving her a chance. Our country needs to give all young people better chances because every society is only as good as its ability to successfully renew itself. And now I must leave you to visit my favourite resident, Miss Ethel Stones."

"Good luck, Doctor. I trust you are wearing your bulletproof vest."

CHAPTER 19

George Rampling had rarely visited The Tip in the past. In his view when things were running smoothly why intervene? This especially applied to someone like himself who was approaching retirement, but things were no longer normal and on this particular Friday he had to visit yet again. The reason for his visit also posed a potential upset.

George drove into the compound's parking area shortly after 9 a.m.

Mollie Knowles noticed his arrival and called over to Jack Sugden: "Rampling is here again, Jack!"

Jack left his usual post after making sure that Dimitri and Stacie were in position. He arrived at the office door just as George Rampling was about to enter.

"Good morning, sir. Good to see you again."

George made no response to the greeting – he was obviously in a serious mood. Once they were inside the office it soon became clear why.

"Have either of you read the local paper this morning?"

Mollie answered, "I've got a copy in my bag, Mr Rampling. Can I get it for you?" George had been hoping that Mollie and Jack would have been forewarned about the news he had to give them.

"No, thank you, Mrs Knowles. There a report in today's edition that is entirely relevant for once, and I'm afraid I am the bringer of bad news because, you see, at the latest council meeting the councillors agreed that this recycling facility must close at the end of the month."

George looked from one staff member to the other; neither seemed surprised.

"Where will people dispose of their waste, Mr Rampling?" Mollie asked the question in a clear, steady voice.

"I'm afraid they will have to take it to the Stafford facility."

"But that's miles away."

"Yes, that is correct, Mr Sugden, and my main worry is that they will dump it in the countryside."

"What about our jobs, Mr Rampling?"

"Well, you will both receive a redundancy payment, of course, Mrs Knowles."

Mollie's eyes narrowed. "I reckon they've chosen this site because we have workers on zero-hours contracts, plus the fact that one full-time worker will definitely never return and another will be laid up for ages."

"You could well be correct, Mrs Knowles; I know for a fact that Tobias Argent has been following developments here. Anyway, I thought it better if I came to tell you myself, but now I must visit the site in Stafford to make sure it can take extra loads. I'll leave it to you to inform the temporary staff."

"Will you tell them or shall I, Jack?" Mollie asked when George Rampling had departed.

"You'll do it better than me, Mollie, but I'll be here with you in support. Perhaps we'd best leave it till closing time."

Mollie had to smile because, at last, Jack would be present when a difficult announcement was required.

The office phone rang at eleven thirty when Mollie was having her break; Nora was on the line.

"Morning, Mollie. Have you read today's *Moorland Observer*?"

"I was just about to, Nora; is there something special?"

"The Tip is all over the front page – it's due for closure."

"Actually I know that, Nora; the big boss told me and Jack earlier."

"But you'll lose contact with that handsome foreign chap, won't you? But, mind you, you will make a saving on that expensive mouthwash you told me about and the extra visits to your hairdresser."

"Well, thank you, Nora, and now, if you don't mind, I'll read the paper for myself."

Mollie rang off and fetched her bag. She was fishing out the paper when Jack joined her.

"Look at this, Jack." Mollie held up the front page.

Jack could read the headline without his reading glasses: 'Chelford Tip to Close'.

Mollie scanned the report and selected a short paragraph to read out: "Local MP Tobias Argent praised the council for taking a difficult but important decision; he also praised staff at The Tip for their fine service over the years. 'Chelford Town Recycling Centre staff have played a major part in preserving cleanliness standards in the town for over twenty years, but of course things move on and the facility at Stafford, which will receive immediate investment, will provide improved standards based on the latest recycling procedures.'"

Mollie lowered the paper and looked at Jack. "I know a procedure where we could recycle a hot poker."

"Really, Mollie, where would that be?"

"Up Argent's arse."

At closing time Jack brought Stacie and Dimitri to the office.

"Mrs Knowles has some important information for you both."

'Well, thank you, Jack,' Mollie thought to herself, but she faced the twosome calmly.

"We were told this morning that The Tip will close down very soon, so I'm afraid your jobs will go."

Mollie and Jack were both surprised by Stacie and Dimitri's reactions. Mollie had expected gloom and despondency; she received only smiles.

Stacie spoke up first: "I've been offered a permanent job as a carer, Mrs Knowles."

Dimitri voiced his reaction too: "I've decided to return to Romania; my wife is pregnant and our baby is due shortly."

Mollie was shocked.

"You never told us you are married, Dimi; you always said you were sending money home to your parents."

"That is true, Mrs Knowles. You see, my wife, Christina,

lives with my parents. Our baby is due in six weeks' time but I can continue here till the end of the month if you want."

Later, when Mollie was at home, she scanned the rest of the newspaper and it was no surprise when she read that Town End Care Home was also due to close. What was not reported, however, was the fact that Syd Fawkes had decided not to renew the lease on The Red Lion. But all was not lost because a national chain of bars and restaurants had made a successful bid for The Red Lion and had offered Syd the post of manager. He had accepted a short-term contract, under the terms of which he had to ensure the chain made a specific profit in one financial year. Syd doubted it was possible, but at least he would not be bankrupt in the short term. He had even made a start at appointing some staff, including Stacie Holt, who had received glowing references from both the Matron at the Town End Care Home and from Jack Sugden at The Tip.

CHAPTER 20

June Bailey and Val Davies were about to leave the Town End Care Home for the last time. All the residents, who had survived the turmoil, had been found placements in other homes. Ethel Stones had been the last to leave. She had moaned continuously as June had wheeled her to a waiting ambulance, but even she had not been able to halt the process. Dr Priest had been present as his least favourite patient left his care. June offered him a final cup of strong black coffee as a parting gift. So for the last time they both sat in Matron's office, this time to contemplate their futures.

"It's all right for you, Doctor – you still have a job, and without your most difficult patient too."

Julian Priest knew she was right, so he tried to be as sensitive as possible. "I'm sure you have some exciting plans for your retirement, Matron."

His affirmative attempt fell flat: "I haven't a clue what I shall do, Doctor."

He sipped his coffee in response and remembered his assessment of life in general. People depended, in his view, on establishing and keeping a sense of personal identity; many, especially those from backgrounds lacking love, had considerable problems accomplishing a secure lifestyle. His career had been littered with patients showing signs of mental illness – problems for which, he recognised, he had not enough knowledge. Many of these patients had become drug users or felons or both.

Doctor Priest knew that even persons considered normal

often had to confront changes in life that threatened their self-esteem, and he recognised that June Bailey was facing one such personal drama.

He drank the rest of his coffee before standing and offering her his hand. "Goodbye, Matron," he said before adding, "I wish you a long and happy retirement."

June shook his hand and, despite the tears in her eyes, she looked into his face. "Goodbye, Doctor. It has been a privilege to work with you."

Julian turned and left her realm for the last time.

The same day June faced another terminal farewell. She and Val both stopped before they went to their cars.

"Well, Mrs Davies, here we are at the last goodbye."

"Don't say that please, Matron – I'm sure we have lots of living left in us."

June managed a smile. "Yes, of course, I'm sure we have."

Their feet crunched on the gravel as they took their separate ways.

EPITAPH

Pete Fenton was dead. George Rampling communicated the sad news to Mollie Knowles at The Tip on the day of its closure. Mollie and Jack were now sitting in silence in the Portakabin trying to come to terms with their collapsing world.

All the waste had now been removed and Mollie's final task would be to transfer all remaining data to the local authority.

Jack attempted to accept their situation: "Well, Mollie, this is it, I suppose."

"It is, Jack. It would have been upsetting enough without the news about Pete."

"Indeed it would, Mollie, but the Grim Reaper visits us all in time, you know. When your time comes will you choose landfill or incineration?"

His colleague placed two fingers of her right hand on her chin as though deliberating deeply. "Well, Jack, I was never one for lying about in damp places, so I think I'll take the warmer option. How about you?"

Jack answered without a pause: "Oh, I'll leave it to the family. They'll go with the cheapest estimate, I've no doubt, but I may choose to disappear into the ether as our former colleague Winston Green appears to have done."

They looked at each other and simultaneously they both managed a humourless smile.